PRAISE FOR THE *SISTERS GRIMM* SERIES:

New York Times Bestseller
Oppenheim Toy Portfolio Platinum Award
Kirkus Best Fantasy Book
A *Real Simple* magazine "Must-Have"

"Mystery meets fairy tale." —The CBS *Early Show*

"Enormously entertaining . . . takes the fractured fairy-tale
genre to new heights." —*Time Out New York Kids*

"Adventure, laughs, and surprises kept me eagerly turning the
pages." —R. L. Stine, author of the *Goosebumps* series

"Kids will love Sabrina and Daphne's adventures as
much as I did." —Sarah Michelle Gellar
(Buffy on *Buffy the Vampire Slayer*)

★ "Features both a pair of memorable young sleuths and a mad-
cap plot." —*Kirkus Reviews*, starred review

"Readers will have trouble putting this novel down."
—*The Dallas Morning News*

THE SISTERS GRIMM

· BOOK ONE ·

✷ THE FAIRY-TALE DETECTIVES ✷

MICHAEL BUCKLEY

PICTURES BY PETER FERGUSON

AMULET BOOKS

New York

The Library of Congress has cataloged the
hardcover edition of this book as follows:
Buckley, Michael.
The sisters Grimm, book one :
the fairy-tale detectives / Michael Buckley.
p. cm.
Summary: Orphans Sabrina and Daphne Grimm are sent to live with an
eccentric grandmother whom they have always believed to be dead.
ISBN 978-0-8109-5925-5
[1. Sisters—Fiction. 2. Orphans—Fiction. 3. Grandmothers—Fiction.
4. Monsters—Fiction.] I. Title.
PZ7+
[Fic]—dc22
2005011784

paperback ISBN 978-0-8109-9322-8

Originally published in hardcover by Amulet Books in 2005
Text copyright © 2007 Michael Buckley
Illustrations copyright © 2007 Peter Ferguson

Designed by Jay Colvin

Printed and bound in U.S.A.
24 23 22 21 20 19 18 17 16 15

Amulet Books are available at special discounts when purchased in quantity for premiums and promotions as well as fundraising or educational use. Special editions can also be created to specification. For details, contact specialsales@abramsbooks.com or the address below.

THE ART OF BOOKS SINCE 1949

115 West 18th Street
New York, NY 10011
www.abramsbooks.com

In memory of my grandparents,
Basil and Relda Gandee

ACKNOWLEDGMENTS

I'd like to thank my editor, Susan Van Metre at Amulet Books, whose guidance helped me find the book inside my idea; my agent, Alison Fargis of the Stonesong Press, for taking a chance on me; Joseph Deasy, who was honest enough to tell me when my writing stunk; my love, Alison, for telling me when Joe was wrong; Jonathan Flom, for all his support over the years; Joe Harris, for being a good friend; my parents, Michael and Wilma, for filling our house with books even when the checking account was empty; and Daisy, who was patient when I was too busy writing to take her for a walk.

THE SISTERS GRIMM

THE FAIRY-TALE DETECTIVES

THE DENSE FOREST BRANCHES *scratched at their faces and arms, but Sabrina and Daphne couldn't stop running, though they had long since passed the point of exhaustion. Fear was fueling each step now.*

Another thunderous bellow rang in the distance, followed by the terrible sound of falling trees and shrieking animals.

"We have to find a way to stop it," Daphne cried between gasps.

Sabrina knew her little sister was right. But how? They were two children versus a vicious monster.

"I'll think of something," Sabrina said, dragging her sister behind an enormous oak tree for a much-needed rest. Sabrina squeezed her sister's hand to reassure her, while she forced oxygen into her own burning lungs. Her words were empty. She didn't have a plan. The only thing going on in her head was the thumping of blood roaring through her eardrums. But it made no difference. It had found them. Splintering wood and damp soil rained from the sky as the tree they stood next to was violently uprooted.

The two girls looked up into the horrible face above them and felt hot breath blow through their hair.

What's happened to our lives? *Sabrina wondered. When had their world become unrecognizable? And what had happened to her, the eleven-year-old girl who only two days ago had been just an orphan on a train?*

1
TWO DAYS AGO

'm going to die of boredom here, Sabrina Grimm thought as she looked out the train window at Ferryport Landing, New York.

The little town in the distance seemed to be mostly hills and trees next to the cold, gray Hudson River. A few two- and three-story brownstone buildings huddled around what appeared to be the town's only street. Beyond it were endless acres of evergreen forest. Sabrina could see no movie theaters, malls, or museums, and felt using the word *town* to describe Ferryport Landing was a bit of a stretch.

Worse than the town was the weather. It was raining, and rain always made Sabrina melancholy. She tucked her long blond hair behind her ear and turned her head away from the window, promising herself that she would be strong and not let her sister see her cry. She had to be the strong one; after all, she was almost twelve years old.

Not that Daphne would have noticed her tears. Sabrina's seven-year-old sister had had her face pressed against the window throughout the two-hour trip. Daphne had marveled at each ugly little spot on the map they rolled through, taking a break from the view only to ask the occasional question about their destination.

"Do they have bagels in Ferryport Landing, Ms. Smirt?" Daphne now asked the woman sitting across from them. Ms. Minerva Smirt was the girls' caseworker. She was a pinch-lipped, humorless woman in her late fifties. She had had her hooked nose buried in a book for the entire train ride. Sabrina knew she was reading only so she wouldn't have to talk to them. Ms. Smirt looked up at Daphne with an annoyed scowl and sighed as if the question was more than she could bear.

"Of course they have bagels. They have bagels everywhere," Ms. Smirt snapped.

"Not on the moon," Daphne replied matter-of-factly as she returned her gaze to the window.

Ms. Smirt snarled, which caused Sabrina to snicker. Watching Daphne drive Ms. Smirt crazy was one of Sabrina's favorite pastimes. Smirt had made a mistake when she chose a career working with children, Sabrina thought, especially since she didn't seem to like them. Ms. Smirt complained whenever she had to touch their sticky hands or wipe their runny noses, and reading bedtime stories was completely out of the question. She seemed to especially dislike the Grimm sisters and had labeled them rude, uncooperative, and a couple of know-it-alls. So, Sabrina was sure it was Ms. Smirt's personal mission to get the girls out of the orphanage and into a foster home. So far she had failed miserably. She'd sent them to live with people who were usually mean and occasionally crazy, and who had used them as maids, house sitters, or just plain ignored them. But this time she had gone too far. This time Ms. Smirt was sending them to live with a dead woman.

"I hope you don't bother your grandmother with all these ridiculous questions!" Ms. Smirt said curtly, which was how she said most things to Sabrina and Daphne. "She is old and cannot handle a lot of trouble."

"She's dead! I've already told you a million times, our grandmother is dead!" said Sabrina.

"We did a background check, Sally," Ms. Smirt replied. "She is who she says she is."

"My name is Sabrina." Sabrina sighed.

"Whatever. The orphanage would not release you into just anyone's custody," said Ms. Smirt.

"Oh really? How about Ms. Longdon, who swore her toilet was haunted?" said Sabrina.

"Everyone has their quirks."

"Or Mr. Dennison, who made us sleep in his truck?" Daphne chimed in.

"Some people love the great outdoors."

"Mr. and Mrs. Johnson handcuffed us to a radiator!" Sabrina cried.

"Dwell on the negative if you choose," said Ms. Smirt. "But you should be grateful. There is not much of a demand for rude little girls. Imagine how embarrassed I was when I heard what you said to the Keatons!"

"They locked us in their house for two weeks so they could go on a cruise to Bora-Bora," Sabrina said.

"I think it was the Bahamas," Daphne said.

"It was Bermuda, and at least they brought you back some nice T-shirts from their trip," said Ms. Smirt. "Anyway, it is all water under the bridge now. We found a *real* relative who is actually eager to take you into her home. But to be honest, girls, even if she was an imposter I would hand you over to her. We have run out of families who want you." With that, Ms. Smirt put her nose back into her book. Sabrina looked up at the title. It was called *How to Get the Love You Want.*

"What's an imposter?" Daphne asked, not bothering to turn her head away from the view through the window.

"It means someone who is pretending to be someone she's not," Sabrina said as she watched the rain outside. It had been raining the day her parents disappeared. That was over a year and a half ago, but it still made her heart ache. She remembered rushing home that afternoon with a report card safely tucked inside her raincoat. Excited about her As in math and English and her B in Science (and a little disappointed by her C-minus in gym), she had proudly taped it to the refrigerator for everyone to see. It had seemed odd that her parents weren't home from work, but Sabrina didn't worry until Daphne's kindergarten teacher called to find out why no one had picked up the little girl. That night the girls slept in their parents' bed, waiting for them to come home as thunder and lighting crashed in the sky around their apartment. When the social worker came three days later to take them away, it was still raining, and Sabrina's report card was still hanging on the refrigerator awaiting its praise. For all Sabrina knew, it was still there.

The police had started an investigation. They searched the family's New York City apartment for clues. They interviewed neighbors and coworkers. They dusted for fingerprints and filed reports, but they found nothing. Henry and Veronica

Grimm had simply vanished into thin air. Months later the police found their abandoned car. The only clue was a blood-red handprint on the dashboard. The police assured the girls that the print was not blood, only paint, but they still had no leads. Their investigation had come to a dead end. Meanwhile, the orphanage where the girls had been taken began an investigation of its own, searching for next-of-kin, but came up as empty as the police. No aunts, uncles, grandparents, brothers, sisters, or even distant twice-removed cousins existed. The girls' parents had always told them that they were all the family they would ever need. So naturally, the girls were shocked when a woman claiming to be "Grandma Grimm" applied for custody.

Now the train pulled into the station and Daphne turned away from the window, cupped her hand over Sabrina's ear, and whispered, "Do you think that she could really be our grandmother? Dad said she died before we were born."

"Not a chance," Sabrina said as the train came to a stop. "Don't worry, we'll be gone before the crazy old bat knows what happened."

Passengers got up from their seats and took their bags down from the luggage racks above. They tossed half-read newspapers onto the coffee-stained floor and headed for the doors. A conductor announced that Ferryport Landing was the last stop.

"Ladies, let's go!" Ms. Smirt ordered, causing Sabrina's stomach to flip-flop. She didn't want to meet the imposter posing as her grandmother, but Ms. Smirt wasn't one to argue with. The old crone had a reputation as a pincher and she had left more than a few nasty purple bruises on back-talking orphans. Sabrina stood up on her seat, dragged their two tiny suitcases down from the storage racks above, and followed Ms. Smirt and Daphne off the train.

The late November rain was bitingly cold. Daphne began to shiver, so Sabrina wrapped her arm around her sister's shoulders and held her tightly as they stood with Ms. Smirt on the crowded platform.

"When you meet her you had better be polite or there is going to be trouble," Ms. Smirt said. "No sass, no back talk, stand up straight, and act like young ladies for once, or so help me I'll—"

"Ms. Smirt?" A voice interrupted the caseworker's threat. The girls looked up to find a chubby old woman standing in front of them. She was dressed in an ankle-length, navy blue dress with a white knitted shawl around her shoulders. Her long, gray hair was streaked with red, hinting at its original color, and she wore it tightly tucked under a matching navy blue hat with an appliqué of a big fuzzy sunflower in the middle. Her face was a collection of wrinkles and sagging skin. Nevertheless, there was something youthful about it. Perhaps it was the old woman's red cheeks and clear, green eyes.

Next to her stood the skinniest man Sabrina had ever seen. He had a full head of untamed platinum hair and enormous, watery eyes buried beneath eyebrows that were in desperate need of a trim. He wore a dark pinstriped suit that was several sizes too big and held a wide umbrella in one hand and his hat in the other.

Ms. Smirt gave the girls a hard pinch on the shoulder, which acted as a warning to behave, and, Sabrina suspected, a last opportunity to inflict some pain.

"Yes, Mrs. Grimm. It's us," Ms. Smirt said, forcing her usual frown into a smile.

"Sabrina? Daphne?" the woman cried with a hint of a German accent. "Oh, you are both so beautiful. What little darlings! I'm your Grandmother Grimm." She wrapped her chubby arms around the girls and hugged them tightly. The girls squirmed to escape. But the old woman was like an over-affectionate octopus hugging them and kissing them on their heads and shoulders.

"Mrs. Grimm, it's so nice to meet you," Ms. Smirt interrupted. Mrs. Grimm raised herself up to her full height, which wasn't very high, and cocked her eyebrow at the caseworker. Sabrina could have sworn she saw the old woman smirk.

"It's nice to meet you, too," said Mrs. Grimm.

"I am just so thrilled to have helped you and the girls reunite."

"Oh, I'm sure you are," said the old woman, turning her back on the caseworker and giving the girls a wink. She placed a hand on each girl's shoulder and turned them toward her companion.

"Girls, this is Mr. Canis. He helps me take care of our house and other matters. He lives with us, too, and he'll be helping me look after you," she said.

Daphne and Sabrina stared up into the old man's gaunt face. He was so skinny and frail-looking that it seemed as though the umbrella he was holding would collapse on him at any moment. He nodded at the girls then handed Mrs. Grimm the umbrella, picked up the suitcases, and walked down the platform toward the parking lot.

"Well, girls, this is good-bye," said Ms. Smirt as her eyes darted to the open train door.

She stepped forward and limply hugged Daphne, whispering something in her ear that made the little girl cringe. Then she hooked Sabrina in her uncomfortable embrace.

"Let's make this the last time we see each other," the caseworker snarled into Sabrina's ear.

"Good luck, Mrs. Grimm," Ms. Smirt said as she released Sabrina and reached out to shake the hand of the old woman, who looked as if the caseworker were trying to give her something smelly and dead. Ms. Smirt, sensing disapproval, hemmed and hawed for a moment and quickly reboarded the train without looking back. The doors shut and the train pulled away, back to New York City. As happy as Sabrina was to be rid of Ms. Smirt, she realized that their caseworker had left them in the care of a complete stranger.

Mrs. Grimm's barrage of kisses continued all the way down the platform to the parking lot where Mr. Canis was waiting for them beside the oldest car Sabrina had ever seen. Dingy and covered in rust, it squealed and protested when Mr. Canis opened the back door and the girls crawled inside.

"Is this safe?" Sabrina asked as Mr. Canis and the old woman settled into their seats.

"It got us here." The old woman laughed. "I suppose it will get us back."

The car sputtered, backfired, and then roared to life, belching a black fog out of its tailpipe. The engine was an orchestra of gears grinding so loudly that Sabrina thought she might go deaf. Daphne had already plugged her fingers into her ears.

Mrs. Grimm turned to the girls and shouted, "Put on your seat belts!"

"What?" Sabrina shouted back.

"What?!" the old woman asked.

"I can't hear you!" Sabrina yelled.

"More than six!" the old woman replied.

"Six what?" Sabrina screamed.

"Probably!" The old woman laughed, turning back around.

Sabrina sighed. Daphne took her fingers out of her ears just long enough to hold up the torn straps of her seat belt. Sabrina rolled her eyes and then looked for hers. She reached down into the ripped-up seats and pulled out a filthy old rope.

"I told you to put on your seat belt!" Mrs. Grimm said.

"This?!" Sabrina shouted, holding up the rope.

"Yes, yes! Here!" The old woman leaned into the backseat and tied the torn straps of Daphne's seat belt to Sabrina's filthy rope so tightly the girls could barely breathe.

"There, snug as a bug in a rug!" the old woman hollered.

"I love dolphins, too!" Daphne exclaimed.

"Not since I hurt my toes!" Mrs. Grimm shouted.

Sabrina put her face in her hands and groaned.

They drove through the little town, which consisted of a two-lane road bordered by a couple of antiques stores, a bicycle shop, a police station, the Ferryport Landing Post Office, a restaurant named Old King Cole's, a toy store, and a beauty parlor. Mr. Canis made a left turn at the town's one and only stoplight and within seconds they were cruising out of the town proper and into what Mrs. Grimm called Ferryport Landing's "farm country." As far as Sabrina could tell, the only crop this town grew was mud.

Mrs. Grimm's house sat far up on a tree-speckled hill fifteen minutes away from the closest neighbor. It was short and squat, much like its owner, and had two stories, a wraparound porch, and small windows with bright blue shutters. Fat green shrubs lined the cobblestone path that led to the front door. It all would have looked cozy, but just behind the house loomed the forest—its branches hanging over the little roof as if the trees were preparing to swallow the house whole.

"You live in a dollhouse," Daphne declared, and Mrs. Grimm smiled.

But Sabrina wasn't amused. The place was creepy and she felt as if she was being watched. She squinted to see into the dense trees, but if anyone was spying they were well hidden.

"Why do you live all the way out here?" she asked. New York City was a place where everyone lived on top of each other, and that was exactly how Sabrina liked it. Living out in the middle of nowhere was dangerous and suspicious.

"Oh, I like the quiet," said Mrs. Grimm. "It's nice not to hear the honking of horns."

And there's no one to hear the screaming of children up here, Sabrina thought to herself.

Mr. Canis unlocked the car's huge musty trunk, pulled out the two tiny suitcases, and led everyone to the front door. The old woman followed closely behind, fumbling with her handbag until she fished out what looked like the largest key ring in the world. Hundreds of keys were attached to it, each different from the others: skeleton keys made from what looked like crystal, ancient brass keys, bright new silver ones in many sizes, and several that didn't look like keys at all.

"Wow! That's a lot of keys," Daphne said.

"That's a lot of locks," Sabrina added as she eyed the front door. It must have had a dozen bolts of all shapes and sizes.

Mrs. Grimm ignored the comment and flipped through the key ring, inserting one key after another into the locks until she had unlocked them all. Then she rapped her knuckles on the door three times and said, "We're home."

Daphne looked up at her sister for an explanation but Sabrina had none. Instead, she twirled her finger around her ear and mouthed the word *crazy*. The little girl giggled.

"Let me take your coats, *lieblings*," Mrs. Grimm said as they entered the house and she closed the door behind them, turning the locks one after another.

"*Liebling*?" Daphne asked.

"It means *sweetheart* in German," the old woman said. She

opened the coat closet door and several books tumbled to her feet. Mr. Canis quickly restacked them for her.

"Girls, I must warn you. I'm not much of a housekeeper," Mrs. Grimm said. "We'll have dinner in about an hour," she said to Mr. Canis, who picked up the girls' suitcases and headed for the stairs.

"Ladies, let me give you the grand tour." She led them into the living room. It was enormous, a much larger room than seemed possible in a cottage so small. Each wall was lined with bookshelves, stuffed with more books than Sabrina had ever seen. Stacks of them also sat on the floor, the tables, and every other surface. A teapot perched precariously on a stack that looked as if it would fall over at any moment. Books were under the couch cushions, under the carpet. Several giant stacks stood in front of an old television, blocking any chance that someone could watch cartoons. On the spines Sabrina read the strangest titles: *Birds of Oz, The Autobiography of an Evil Queen,* and *Shoes, Toys, and Cookies: The Elvish Handcraft Tradition.*

Mrs. Grimm led them through another door where a dining room table sat littered with books, open and waiting to be read. Sabrina picked one up and rolled her eyes when she read the title: *365 Ways to Cook Dragon.*

The old woman led them from room to room, showing them where she kept the snacks in the white-tiled kitchen and how to get the rickety bathroom door to close. Sabrina pretended to be interested but in reality she secretly "cased the joint." It was a technique she had picked up after spending a year in the foster care system. In each room she noted where the windows and doors were, eyed locks, and paid close attention to creaky floorboards. But it wasn't easy. She kept getting distracted by the odd books and the dozens of old black-and-white photographs that decorated the walls. Most of them were of a much younger Mrs. Grimm and a stocky, bearded man with a wide smile. There were pictures of them hiking in the jungle, standing on an icy glacier, scaling a mountain, and even riding camels in the desert. In some pictures, Mrs. Grimm was carrying a small child in a papoose, while the bearded man stood next to her, proudly beaming at the camera.

Daphne was just as distracted, and when they arrived back in the living room, she walked over to a picture and looked at it closely.

"That was your *opa*, Basil," Mrs. Grimm said wistfully.

"*Opa*?" Daphne asked.

"Grandfather, *liebling*. He passed on about eleven years ago," she said.

"Is that your baby?" Daphne said.

The old lady smiled and studied the picture as if she weren't sure. "That's your papa," she said with a smile. The little girl eyed the photo closely, but Sabrina turned away. Babies all looked the same. An old photo couldn't prove anything.

"Oh, my, I've forgotten the cookies," the old woman said as she dashed to the kitchen. In no time she returned with a plate of warm chocolate-chip cookies. Daphne, of course, happily grabbed one and took a bite.

"These taste just like my mommy's," she exclaimed.

"Where do you think she got the recipe, angel?" Mrs. Grimm said.

Sabrina refused to take a cookie, giving Mrs. Grimm an "I know what you're up to" look. She wasn't going to be bribed with sweets.

Just then, Mr. Canis walked into the room.

"I was about to introduce the girls to Elvis," Mrs. Grimm said to him.

Mr. Canis gave a slight smile, nodded, and walked past them toward the kitchen.

That's a weird man, Sabrina thought as she noted two loud creaks in the middle of the living room floor.

"Is he your boyfriend?" Daphne asked the old woman, who was trying to balance the plate of cookies on top of two uneven stacks of books.

Mrs. Grimm blushed and giggled. "Oh, dear, no. Mr. Canis and I are not courting. We are just good friends," she said.

"What does *courting* mean?" Daphne asked her sister.

"It's an old-fashioned word for dating," Sabrina replied.

Suddenly, there was a great rumbling in the house. Books fell from their shelves, windows shook in their frames, and the tray of cookies slid to the floor before the old woman could catch it. And then something enormous came charging through the room and right at them.

It moved so quickly Sabrina couldn't tell what it was. It pushed over lamps and chairs, leaped over an ottoman, and knocked the terrified girls to the ground. Sabrina screamed, sure they were about to be eaten when, much to her surprise, a gooey tongue licked her cheek. She opened her eyes and looked up at the friendly face of a giant dog.

"Elvis, please, get off of them," Mrs. Grimm said, half commanding and half laughing at the Great Dane. "He gets very excited around new people." The enormous dog gave one last lick to Sabrina's face, leaving a long trail of drool, before sitting down next to the old woman, panting and wagging his immense tail.

"This is Elvis. He's a member of our little family and completely harmless if he likes you," said Mrs. Grimm, scratching the beast on his immense head. The dog licked the old woman on the cheek.

"And if he doesn't?" Sabrina asked as she climbed to her feet. The old woman ignored her question.

Daphne, on the other hand, jumped up and threw her arms around the dog. "Oh, I love him! He's so cute!" She laughed as she covered the dog with her own kisses.

"This is the only boyfriend I have." Mrs. Grimm smiled. "And probably the smartest one I've ever had, too. Watch!"

Daphne stepped back and she and Sabrina watched as Mrs. Grimm put her hand out to Elvis. "Elvis, shake," she said, and the dog reached out a huge forepaw and placed it in her hand.

Daphne giggled.

"Play dead," Daphne said hopefully, and the dog fell stiffly over onto his side. The impact dislodged several books from a nearby shelf.

Mrs. Grimm laughed. "You two must be starving after your trip. I suppose I better get started with dinner. I hope spaghetti and meatballs is OK."

"I love spaghetti and meatballs!" Daphne cried as Elvis gave her a fresh lick.

"I know you do," Mrs. Grimm said with a wink. She disappeared into the kitchen, where she began rattling pots and pans.

"I don't like this at all, Daphne," Sabrina said as she wiped off the last of the dog's goo. "Don't get used to this place. We're not going to be here long."

"Stop being a snot," Daphne said as she laid a huge smooch on Elvis. *Snot* was her favorite word lately. "She wouldn't hurt us. She's nice."

"That's why crazy people are so dangerous. You think they're *nice* until they're chaining you up in the garage," Sabrina replied. "And I am not being a snot."

"Yes, you are."

"No, I'm not."

"Yes, you are," Daphne insisted. "Anything is better than living at the orphanage, right?"

Daphne had a point. Sabrina walked over and examined the photograph the old woman claimed was of the girls' father. The rosy-cheeked baby in the photo seemed to stare back at her.

• • •

Mr. Canis had cleared the big oak dining room table of enough books for everyone to eat comfortably. He had left an exceptionally thick volume entitled *Architecture for Pigs* on Daphne's chair so the little girl could reach her dinner. As they waited patiently for Mrs. Grimm, who was still making a thunderous racket in the kitchen, Mr. Canis closed his eyes and sat silently. Soon, his stillness began to unnerve Sabrina. Was he a mute? Was there something wrong with him? In New York City, everyone talked, or rather, everyone yelled at everyone, all the time. They never sat quietly with their eyes closed when people were around. It was rude.

"I think he's dead," Daphne whispered after staring at him for some time.

Suddenly, Mrs. Grimm came through the door with a big copper pot and placed it on the table. She rushed back into the kitchen and returned with a plate of salad and set it in front of Mr. Canis. As soon as the plate hit the table the old man opened his eyes and began to eat.

"How did you know I like spaghetti? It's my favorite!" Daphne said happily.

"I know lots of things about you, *liebling*. I am your *oma*," Mrs. Grimm replied.

"*Oma*?" Sabrina asked. "What's this weird language you keep speaking?"

"It means *grandmother* in German. That's where our family is from," Mrs. Grimm answered.

"My family is from New York City," Sabrina said stiffly.

The old woman smiled a sad smile. "Your mama sent me letters from time to time. I know a great deal about you both. In fact, when I stopped getting them I knew that . . ." She sighed.

"That they'd abandoned us?" Sabrina snapped. Suddenly, Sabrina felt as if she might burst into tears. She ducked her head, fighting their escape down her cheeks.

"Child, your mother and father didn't abandon you," Mrs. Grimm cried.

"Mrs. Grimm, I —" Daphne began.

"*Liebling*, I'm not Mrs. Grimm. I'm your grandmother," the old woman said. "You can call me *Grandma* or *Oma*, but never *Mrs. Grimm*, please."

"Can we call you *Granny*? I always wanted a granny," said Daphne. Sabrina kicked her sharply under the table and the little girl winced.

"Of course, I'll be your Granny Relda," the old woman said with a smile, as she took the top off the pot.

Sabrina stared inside. She had never seen spaghetti like this. The noodles were black and the sauce was a bright orange color. It smelled both sweet and spicy at the same time, and the meatballs, which were emerald green, were surely not made from any kind of meat Sabrina had ever had.

"It's a special recipe," Mrs. Grimm said, as she dished some out for Daphne. "The sauce has a little curry in it and the noodles are made with squid ink."

Sabrina was disgusted. There was no way she was going to eat the old woman's weird food. This sicko had lied about being someone's dead grandmother. Who knew what she had yanked from under the kitchen sink and added to the recipe: arsenic, rat poison, clog remover? No, Sabrina wasn't going to eat a noodle. Of course, Daphne dug in with gusto and had already swallowed a third of her plate before Sabrina could warn her.

"So, Mr. Canis says your suitcases felt almost empty. Don't you have any clothes?" Mrs. Grimm asked.

"The police kept them," Daphne said, shoveling a huge fork-ful of noodles into her mouth. "They said they were evidence."

"Kept them? That's crazy! What will they do with them?" She looked at each of them and finally at Mr. Canis, who shrugged.

"Well, we'll have to go into town and pick you out new wardrobes. We can't have you running around naked all the time, can we? I mean, people will think we're nudists."

Daphne laughed to the point of snorting, but when she saw Sabrina's disapproving face she stopped and stuck her tongue out at her sister.

"I was thinking that we—" Mrs. Grimm started, but Sabrina interrupted.

"Who are you? And don't say you're our grandmother because our grandmother is dead!"

Mrs. Grimm shifted in her seat. Mr. Canis, obviously seeing

the question as his cue to retire, got up, took his empty plate, and exited the room.

"But I am your grandmother, *liebling,*" the old woman replied.

"I said our grandmother is dead. Our father told us she died before we were born."

"Girls, I assure you that I am who I say I am."

"Well, then why did he tell us you died if you didn't?"

"I'm not sure it is time to discuss your father's decisions. We are all just getting settled in and we can talk about it later," Mrs. Grimm said. Her eyes dropped to her lap.

"Well if you really were our grandmother, I would think you'd be happy to discuss it," Sabrina snapped.

"Now is not the time," Mrs. Grimm said softly.

Sabrina leaped up from her seat, sending her fork clanging to the floor. "Fine! I'm tired and want to go to bed."

Mrs. Grimm frowned. "Of course, *liebling.* Your room is upstairs. I will show you—"

"WE'LL FIND IT OURSELVES!"

Sabrina walked around the table, grabbed Daphne's hand, and dragged her from her chair.

"But I'm not done eating!" said Daphne.

"You're never done eating. Let's go!" Sabrina commanded.

She marched through the house and up the stairs with her sister in tow. At the top of the stairs they found a long hallway with five closed doors, two on each side and one at the end of the hallway. Sabrina yanked on the closest one, but it was locked tight. She turned and tried the door behind her. It opened to a bedroom decorated with dozens of wooden tribal masks, wild-eyed and smiling hideously. Two ancient swords were mounted on the wall alongside the masks, and there were pictures of Mrs. Grimm and her husband, Basil, everywhere. Like the ones downstairs, each photo was of a different part of the world. In one picture, Basil was standing at the top of an ancient stone temple; in another, the couple were guiding a gondola through what Sabrina guessed were Venetian canals. She closed the door, realizing that this had to be the old woman's room. She tried the next door.

Inside, Mr. Canis sat cross-legged on the floor, his hands resting on his knees. Several candles lit the nearly empty room, illuminating its sparse furnishings and a small woven mat on the floor. There were no pictures or decorations at all. Mr. Canis opened his eyes and turned to look at the girls, his eyebrows arched.

Sabrina slammed the door without apologizing. "What a nutcase," she muttered. The next door opened to a queen-sized, four-poster bed with their suitcases resting on top. Sabrina pulled Daphne inside and slammed the door.

"That woman is hiding something!" she said.

"You think everyone's hiding something."

"And you would hug the devil if he gave you cookies."

"Well, I like her!" said Daphne. She sat down on the bed and let out a *Harrumph!*

Sabrina looked around the room. It was painted in soft yellow and had a slanted ceiling and a fireplace. A red ten-speed bicycle sat in the corner, an old baseball mitt rested on a desk, and several model airplanes hung from the ceiling. A nightstand sat next to the bed with an alarm clock perched on top. And on every wall were dozens of old photographs. A particularly large one showed two young boys staring out over the Hudson River.

Sabrina went to the window and looked out at the porch roof below. She could probably jump off it and then to the ground, but Daphne might hurt herself.

"Let's give her a chance," Daphne begged.

"A chance to what? Kill us in our sleep? Feed us to that monster dog of hers? No way!" Sabrina said. "While you were shoveling in those meatballs did you ever think that they might be made from the last couple of kids she claimed she was related to?"

Daphne rolled her eyes. "You're gross!"

Suddenly Sabrina heard a faint whistling sound, almost like a flute, coming from outside the window. She peered into the dark forest behind the house. At first she thought she had seen something or someone sitting in a tree, but when she rubbed her eyes for a clearer look there was nothing there. Still, the music continued.

"Where is that coming from?" she said.

And like an answer to her question, a little light flickered outside the window. Sabrina thought it was a lightning bug. It flew up to the window as if it was trying to get a better view of her. It was joined by another light and the two danced around each other, zipping excitedly back and forth in the air.

"Amazing," she said.

Daphne rushed to the window. "They're so pretty," she whispered as dozens more lights joined the original two. Within seconds there were almost a hundred little lights blinking and flashing outside.

Without thinking, Sabrina reached up and unlocked the window. She just wanted to get a closer look, maybe grab a couple to keep in a jar in the room, but as she undid the window's latch, the bedroom door blew open with a crash. Startled, the sisters spun around and found Mr. Canis looming in the doorway.

"Girls, you'll leave that window closed if you know what's good for you!" he growled.

2

r. Canis stomped across the room, pushed the girls aside, and locked the window. The little lights outside flew around, bounced off the glass several times, and buzzed as if in protest. A moment later they were gone, and the whistling sound faded away. Mr. Canis turned and stood over Sabrina.

"You are never to let anyone or anything inside this house," he said in a voice as low and scratchy as an angry dog's.

"It was just some lightning bugs," said Sabrina. Her face was hot and red with shock. Who was this man to think he could tell her what to do?

"No one comes into this house. Do you understand what I have just asked of you?" Mr. Canis said.

The girls nodded.

"Very well. Good night." He stalked out of the room, closing the door behind him. Sabrina stood dumbfounded, trying to comprehend what had just happened.

"What was that all about?" Daphne whispered, but Sabrina said nothing. She didn't want her sister to hear the fear in her voice. Since her parents had run off, Sabrina had had to be the tough one. Her little sister needed to know there was someone strong by her side, even if it meant Sabrina had to pretend sometimes.

There was a knock on the door and Mrs. Grimm entered the room. "It's been a long day, hasn't it?"

"Mr. Canis yelled at us," Daphne cried.

"I heard," the old woman said as she sat down on the bed. "Please don't be too upset by Mr. Canis. He can be a little grouchy from time to time but he has your best interests at heart. Believe me, *lieblings*, we are both very happy to have you here, but there are a few rules you have to follow . . ." she said, pausing as she looked into Sabrina's face, ". . . and I know that what I tell you might not make a lot of sense but the rules are in place for a reason.

"First, never let anyone or anything into this house without asking Mr. Canis or me if it is OK," she said. Her tone was stern and serious and no longer that of the sweet, loving old lady with the funky spaghetti.

Mrs. Grimm took the girls' hands in her own. "Second, there is a room down the hall that is locked. It's locked for a reason and I ask that you stay away from it for the time being. You might hear some unusual noises coming from inside, but just ignore them. Do you understand?" she asked.

The girls nodded.

"As for the rest of the house, feel free to explore. You'll notice there are plenty of books to keep you occupied."

"Really? Books? I didn't notice," Sabrina said sarcastically.

"If worse comes to worst we can always dig out that old TV," Mrs. Grimm continued, as if Sabrina hadn't spoken. She got up from the bed and crossed to the door. She turned to smile at them one last time. "Who wants pancakes in the morning?"

Daphne's face lit up. "I do!"

"Are you warm enough? Do you need anything to sleep in?"

The little girl opened one of the suitcases and pulled out two extra large T-shirts tnat read "Bermuda Is for Lovers."

"No, we have these," she said.

"Very good," Mrs. Grimm said. "Good night, don't let the bedbugs bite."

"She's nice," said Daphne when the old lady was gone.

Sabrina clenched her fists. "It's all an act. That woman is hiding something and we aren't sticking around to find out what it is. Get some sleep. We're running away—tonight."

• • •

Sabrina lay in bed staring at the ceiling, listening to her hungry belly grumble, and planning their getaway. With a little luck she and Daphne could hide in a neighbor's garage for a couple of days and then hitchhike back to New York City. After that, she didn't know. In the past they had just gone back to the orphanage, but this time Ms. Smirt might act on her threat to skin them alive. The next place she sent them would be a million times worse. The girls were on their own now.

"We have to go," Sabrina whispered to her sister when she was sure the rest of the house was asleep.

Daphne sat up and rubbed her eyes but said nothing. Her heartbroken face said it all. *Why is she acting like such a baby?* Sabrina wondered. Running away wasn't exactly a new experience for the two of them. The sisters Grimm had pulled off several daring escapes from foster parents in the last year and a half. They had tied bedsheets together and climbed out of the Mercers' window one night, feeding their pit bull, Diablo, meatballs stuffed with cayenne pepper to keep him busy. And after the Johnsons had ordered pizza, the girls had slipped into the backseat of the delivery boy's car and were miles away before he even noticed them. Mrs. Grimm was no different than any of the other lunatics they had run away from. Eventually, Daphne would understand.

When they were dressed and packed, Sabrina slowly opened the door and looked out into the hallway. It was empty—and as the two girls crept out with their tiny suitcases, she used her skills to the fullest. They tiptoed down the stairs, being careful to step close to the wall to avoid making them creak. At the bottom, Sabrina slowly opened the closet door so the latch wouldn't click and the stack of books inside wouldn't fall over and wake the house. She snatched their coats and the girls put them on, then walked to the front door. Sabrina was just thinking that this was the easiest escape they had ever made when she tried to turn the knob. The door was locked. When she looked closely she noticed something unusual that she had not noticed before.

"There's a keyhole on this side, too," she said. They were locked in. "We have to find another way out."

The girls crept through the house, doing their best to avoid knocking over any books. They tried all the windows only to discover each had been nailed shut. They found a back door off the kitchen but it, too, had a lock on the inside.

"Let's go back to bed," said Daphne.

"We have to get her keys," said Sabrina.

The little girl cocked an eyebrow. "How are we going to do that? She has them."

"You'll see," Sabrina whispered.

The sisters found their way back up the stairs to Mrs. Grimm's room. The door was shut tight, but Sabrina was happy to find there were no locks on it. She slowly turned the knob and it swung open.

The old woman's room was scary at night. The tribal masks they had seen after dinner were even creepier in the dark, and the swords mounted on the wall flashed a ghostly light around the room. Mrs. Grimm was asleep in her bed, unaware of their presence, and snoring loudly. Daphne had the same annoying habit.

"Where are they?" Daphne said, only to have Sabrina's hand clamp over her mouth.

"Keep quiet," Sabrina whispered. The old woman turned in bed but stayed asleep.

Sabrina scanned the room and spied the keys glinting in the moonlight, on a table on the far side of the bed. She looked at Daphne, pointed to herself with her free hand, and then pointed to the keys. Daphne nodded and Sabrina let go of her mouth.

Sabrina took a small step forward to test for creaky floor-boards. *This is going to be easy,* she thought, but as her confidence was building, she noticed that Daphne had taken an interest in one of the masks on the wall. The little girl took it off its nail and held it against her face.

"Don't do that!" Sabrina whispered.

"Why not?"

"Put it back. Now!"

The little girl frowned and placed it back on its nail. "There! Are you happy?" she whispered. A split second later the mask fell off the wall, landed with a loud clunk, and rolled toward the bed. Both girls dove to the floor as Mrs. Grimm sat up.

"Who's there?" she asked. "Oh, it's you. What are you doing down there?"

Sabrina was sure they had been caught, but the old woman leaned over, picked up the mask, and set it on the nightstand. "I'll have Mr. Canis give you a new nail tomorrow."

Then she fell back onto her pillow and within minutes was snoring as loudly as ever.

"You did that on purpose," Sabrina seethed.

"Whatever," Daphne whispered, and rolled her eyes.

Sabrina scowled. Was her little sister trying to sabotage their escape?

Sabrina crept around the bed to the table, picked up the keys, and then tiptoed back across the room and into the hallway with her sister behind her. Downstairs, she quietly went to work on the front door lock. There were so many keys, it took a long time to find the right one, but eventually she heard a loud thunk. The girls waited for several moments, sure that someone had heard, but when no sound came from upstairs, they scurried outside.

"Good-bye, dollhouse," Daphne said sadly as she ran her hand lovingly across the door.

"We'll go through the woods. We don't want anyone to see us on the road and call the police," Sabrina said, grabbing her sister's hand and leading her around to the back of the house.

The girls looked into the dark forest in front of them. Crooked limbs twisted and turned in painful directions. Sabrina had the sense that the trees were horrible, mutated guardians, threatening anyone who stepped onto their land. A cold wind whipped through the branches, bending some of the smaller trees over and making a breathy moan. Sabrina knew it was just her overactive imagination, but the woods seemed to be alive and reaching out for them.

Behind them, the girls heard a surprised yelp and Elvis suddenly appeared. He trotted over and planted himself between them and the trees. His happy face was now serious.

"Go away, Elvis," Sabrina commanded, but the dog refused.

"See, he doesn't think we should go, either," said Daphne as she wrapped her arms around the big dog and kissed him on the mouth. But Sabrina had made up her mind. She pulled her sister away and into the forest, with Elvis trotting after them.

Inside the trees, everything was deadly still. There were no scurrying animals, rustling branches, or snapping twigs. Even the whistling breeze had faded away. It was if someone had turned the volume down on the world.

Suddenly, a high-pitched note filled the air. It seemed to come from deep inside the woods.

"What was that?" Daphne said.

Sabrina shrugged. "Probably the wind."

Elvis whined loudly. Then he rushed to Sabrina and clamped his jaw onto her coat sleeve, trying to yank her back toward the house. She pulled away. The girls hurried on with the dog close behind, barking warnings.

Just ignore him. He'll go back when he gets bored, Sabrina said to herself as something zipped past her eye. She turned to get a better look and saw it was a firefly, just like the ones that had been outside their window earlier that night.

"Look, Daphne. Here's the big menacing invader Mr. Skin-and-Bones was afraid would get into the house." Sabrina laughed. The little bug fluttered around her head and then circled her body.

"Pretty," Daphne said, only to find that she had her own little bug floating nearby. "I've got one, too!"

Elvis let out a very low growl.

"What's the matter, buddy?" Daphne said as she scratched the dog's ears. This did nothing to sooth Elvis. The Great Dane howled menacingly and lunged at the lights with snapping teeth.

"Hush up!" Sabrina ordered, but the dog wouldn't stop. He was going to wake Mrs. Grimm and Mr. Canis if he didn't calm down.

"Sabrina," Daphne said. The nervousness in the little girl's voice pulled Sabrina's attention away from the dog. Daphne had her hand over her nose, but what startled Sabrina was the fear in the little girl's eyes. She had seen the same look the morning after their parents disappeared, when they had woken up in their parents' bed, alone.

"What's wrong?" Sabrina asked.

"It just bit me," Daphne said as she removed her hand from her nose. It was covered in blood. Sabrina was shocked. Lightning bugs didn't bite. At least no lightning bugs she had ever heard about. And at that moment, she felt a sting that brought blood to the top of her hand. "Ouch!"

Daphne cried out. "I got bit again!" Blood trickled down her earlobe. Sabrina rushed over and wiped her sister's ear with her sleeve. The two bugs became ten and then a hundred and then a swarm that circled the girls—thousands of angry little lights, zipping back and forth, diving at their heads and arms and lighting up the ugly trees around them. Elvis growled at the bugs, but there was little he could do.

"Cover your face with your hands and run!" Sabrina shouted. The two girls ran as fast as they could, with Elvis at their heels. Sabrina looked back, hoping the bugs weren't following, only to see the swarm close behind and gaining.

In seconds they were stinging the girls again. Daphne cried out and tripped over a tree root. She curled into a ball and tried to hide any exposed skin. Elvis leaped on top of the little girl, doing his best to cover her as the bugs dived, stinging her uncovered hands and legs.

Sabrina had to do something. Elvis couldn't protect Daphne. She waved her hands and screamed at the bugs and they instantly darted in her direction. She turned to run, but before she could take even a step she slammed into something and fell to the ground. It was Mrs. Grimm.

"It's OK, *liebling*," she said.

"We have to run, Mrs. Grimm," Sabrina cried, but the old woman stood calmly, as if she was daring the bugs to come closer. When the swarm was nearly on top of them, the old woman raised her hand to her mouth and blew a soft blue dust into the air. Many of the bugs froze in midflight, falling to the ground like snowflakes. The blue mist took out half of their numbers. The rest regrouped and began to circle the old woman again.

"I have a whole house full of this," Mrs. Grimm shouted. Incredibly, the bugs seemed to weigh their options, and in one mass they darted deep into the woods and disappeared.

"That wasn't very nice!" Mrs. Grimm shouted into the forest. She turned back to Sabrina and extended her hand. "I'll need your help getting Daphne into the house."

• • •

Sabrina was sure the old woman would be furious with them. There was no telling if her craziness could extend to violence. Who could tell what a woman who had swords hanging over her bed was capable of? But Mrs. Grimm didn't seem angry at all. In fact, she looked genuinely concerned.

She asked Sabrina to undress her sister while the old woman rushed into the bathroom and returned with a bottle of calamine lotion and some cotton balls. She applied the lotion to Daphne's stings and tucked the little girl into bed.

"She'll be fine in the morning, maybe itchy, but fine," Mrs.

Grimm said as she handed the calamine lotion to Sabrina. "Pixies are harmless unless you are overwhelmed by them."

"Did you just say *pixies*?" Sabrina asked, unsure if the old woman was joking.

Mrs. Grimm wrapped her arms around her and gave her a big hug. "*Liebling*, it's OK now. You can stop crying."

Sabrina wiped her face and felt the tears on her hand. She hadn't known she was crying.

• • •

In the morning, Sabrina was as hungry as she had ever been. But she was still not going to eat. She'd already looked like a crybaby in front of the old lady. She wasn't about to give up any more ground. By the time the girls heard Mrs. Grimm calling them for breakfast, Sabrina had spent twenty minutes trying to explain her philosophy to her sister.

"You can stay up here if you want, but I'm starving," said Daphne. The idea of skipping a meal was beyond the little girl's imagination.

"We're not eating that woman's food," Sabrina said, her stomach growling. "We can't let her think she's breaking us down. We have to stay strong."

"I have an idea," Daphne said. "Why don't we have breakfast, eat her cookies, play with Elvis, and enjoy the bed. She'll think she's won us over and then one day, when she least expects it, we'll be gone."

Sabrina thought about her sister's plan. She had to admit it was pretty good. She just wished Daphne hadn't sounded so sarcastic when she said it.

The girls got dressed and walked tentatively into the hallway. As they approached the stairs, Sabrina heard something coming from the locked room across from Mrs. Grimm's. It sounded like a voice, but she couldn't be sure. She put her head to the door and the noise stopped.

"Did you hear someone talking in there?" Sabrina asked her sister.

"It was my belly. It's screaming for breakfast." Daphne grabbed Sabrina's hand and dragged her downstairs to the dining room. Much to Sabrina's relief, creepy Mr. Canis was nowhere to be seen. After several moments, Mrs. Grimm came out of the kitchen with a big plate of pancakes.

"I hope everyone likes flapjacks," she sang.

"Yum!" Daphne cheered as the old woman stacked three on her plate, along with a couple of sausage links, then turned to serve Sabrina, whose mouth was watering. Sabrina hadn't had pancakes since her parents disappeared. Her empty belly was telling her to seriously consider Daphne's plan.

"Hold on, *lieblings*. I forgot the syrup," Mrs. Grimm said, rushing back into the kitchen. As soon as she was gone, Daphne looked underneath her pancakes as if she were expecting a buried surprise.

"They're just pancakes," she said.

"You sound disappointed," Mrs. Grimm said, laughing, as she returned with a large gravy boat.

"Well, after last night's spaghetti I thought maybe you cooked like that all the time," Daphne said wistfully.

"Oh, *liebling*, I do." The old woman tilted the gravy boat over Daphne's pancakes and a sticky, bright pink liquid bubbled out. To Sabrina it looked like gelatin that hadn't had time to set. When Daphne saw it her eyes grew as wide as the pancakes on her plate.

"What's that?" she cried.

"Try it," Mrs. Grimm said with a grin.

Naturally, Daphne dug in, greedily wolfing down bite after bite. "It's delicious!" she exclaimed with a mouth full of food.

"It's a special recipe. It has marigolds in it." Mrs. Grimm, proudly poured it onto Sabrina's pancakes before the girl had a chance to refuse. Sabrina looked down at the funky, fizzing sauce. It smelled faintly of peanut butter and mothballs and

Sabrina's stomach did a flip-flop in protest. She dropped her fork and pushed her plate away.

Suddenly, there was a pounding from upstairs.

"So, perhaps we should discuss last night's excitement," said Mrs. Grimm as she sat down at the table and tucked a napkin into the front of her bright green dress. She gazed across at Sabrina and arched a questioning eyebrow.

"It wasn't my idea," Daphne said. Sabrina scowled at this betrayal.

"Well, no harm done. No broken bones or anything," the old woman said.

"Granny, you have some mean bugs in your yard," Daphne said as she poured more of the syrup on her breakfast.

"I know, *liebling*. They sure are mean."

"What is that hammering?" asked Sabrina.

"Mr. Canis is nailing your windows shut," Mrs. Grimm said as she took a bite of her breakfast.

"What?!" the girls said in shocked unison.

"I can't take any chances that something could get into the house or someone might try to get out," the old woman replied over the loud banging.

"So, we're your prisoners?" Sabrina cried.

"Oh, you're just like your *opa*." Mrs. Grimm laughed. "What a flare for the dramatic. Let's put it behind us. Today is a new day with a new adventure. This morning I received a call. There's been an incident that requires our attention. How exciting! You two haven't even been here a full day yet and already we're in the thick of it."

"In the thick of what?" Daphne asked as she placed a fat pat of green butter on her second stack of pancakes.

"You'll see." The old woman got up from her chair, went into the living room, and came back with several shopping bags. She placed them next to the table.

"Mr. Canis went to the store to buy you some clothing, just a couple of things to tide you over until we can go shopping."

Sabrina looked in the bag. Inside were some of the strangest clothes she had ever seen. There were two pairs of bright blue pants that had little hearts and balloons sewn onto them. There were two identical sweatshirts that were as awful as the pants— bright orange with a monkey in a tree on the front. Underneath the monkey were printed the words "Hang in there!"

"You expect us to wear these?" Sabrina moaned.

"Oh, I love them!" Daphne said, pulling the orange monkey sweatshirt out and hugging it like a new doll.

After breakfast, the girls got dressed and looked at their new outfits in the bedroom mirror. Daphne, of course, thought her crazy outfit was the best she had ever had and strutted around like a giddy fashion model. Sabrina, on the other hand, was sure Mr. Canis was trying to punish them for attempting to run away.

"Hurry, girls, we have to get going," Granny called.

"I feel like a movie star," Daphne said as the girls hurried downstairs.

"You look like a mental patient," Sabrina remarked.

• • •

The sisters stood by the door, waiting for the old woman to collect her things. Mrs. Grimm rushed around the house, grabbing books off of shelves and from underneath the couch, creating a tornado of dust that followed her from room to room. When she had collected as many as she could carry, she handed them to Sabrina.

"Almost ready," she sang as she rushed up the stairs.

Sabrina looked down at the top book. It was entitled *Fables and Folklore: The Complete Handbook*. Before she could question the book's purpose, she heard the old woman pull out her keys and unlock the mysterious door upstairs.

"She's going into her secret room," Sabrina whispered to her sister. Daphne's eyes widened and she bit the palm of her hand. For some reason Daphne did this whenever she was overly excited, and though it embarrassed Sabrina, she let it pass. If she tried to curb all of Daphne's odd little quirks, she would never get any sleep.

"I wonder what's in there," Daphne whispered back.

"That's probably where she keeps the bodies of all the other kids she's stolen from the orphanage."

Daphne stuck out her tongue and gave her sister a raspberry.

Sabrina had to admit she was curious about the room. Whenever she was told she couldn't do something, Sabrina found it was all she could think about doing. But the great thing about rules was that you could break them and drive adults crazy.

"Do you hear that?" Daphne asked.

"Yeah, she's talking to someone," Sabrina replied. "Probably Mr. Canis."

Sabrina strained to hear the conversation, but before she could make out anything, she heard Mrs. Grimm leave the room, lock the door, and head back down the stairs.

"Ladies, we're off," she said as she ushered them outside and went to work locking the front door. Then she knocked on the door three times, as she had the day before, but this time she said, "We'll be back."

"Who are you talking to?" Sabrina asked.

"The house," Mrs. Grimm replied, as if this were a perfectly natural thing to do.

Daphne knocked on the door as well. "Good-bye, dollhouse," she said, causing her sister to sigh and roll her eyes.

As they turned to go to the car, Sabrina looked up and nearly stumbled. Mr. Canis wasn't upstairs! He was standing on the path with Elvis at his side. He returned her stare with a look of slight contempt. His gaze unnerved the girl, but no more than the realization that Mrs. Grimm had been talking to herself in her secret room.

"We're ready, Mr. Canis," Mrs. Grimm said, and he nodded. They all climbed into the squeaky car, including Elvis, who laid his huge body across the girls' laps.

"Did you have a chat with our neighbor?" Mrs. Grimm asked Mr. Canis as they all buckled or tied themselves in.

"We began a conversation," the old man grumbled. "But he can be stubborn."

"Well, he'll get used to it eventually, I suppose," Mrs. Grimm replied.

"He doesn't have a history of getting used to things," Mr. Canis said.

Mrs. Grimm sighed and nodded.

"Who are you talking about?" Daphne asked.

"Oh, just a neighbor. Nothing to worry about. You'll meet him soon enough."

Sabrina looked around. She was sure they were miles from the nearest neighbor.

Mr. Canis fired up the engine and the car rocked back and forth violently like a bucking bronco trying to get rid of a cowboy, calming down as they drove out the driveway and through desolate back roads. Sabrina reexamined Ferryport Landing, the world's most boring town. There was little obvious life, except an old dairy cow standing on the side of the road. Mrs. Grimm leaned over and honked, then waved wildly at the cow as they passed. When Daphne giggled about it, the old woman smiled and told her how important it was to be friendly. Meanwhile, Sabrina made the best of the trip by memorizing street names and calculating how long it would take to walk to the train station.

They came to a mailbox with the name *Applebee* marked on it and Mr. Canis turned the car down a long, leaf-covered driveway lined with ancient cedars, pines, and oaks. The car passed a tractor sitting alone on a little hill and pulled over into a clearing where a massive pile of wood and pipes and glass sat surrounded by yellow emergency tape. Mrs. Grimm looked at Mr. Canis and smiled.

"Well, we haven't had to deal with something like this in a while, have we, Mr. Canis?" she asked.

The old man shook his head and helped her out of the car. Once she got on her feet, Mrs. Grimm opened the back door, reached in, and scratched Elvis behind the ears.

"Girls, do you mind if I borrow my boyfriend for a moment?" she asked as she winked at Daphne.

The Great Dane crawled clumsily out of the car, stretched a little, and looked up at the old woman for instructions. She fumbled in her purse and took out a small piece of fabric that she held under the dog's nose. He sniffed it deeply, then rushed over to the huge pile of debris and began hunting through the rubble.

"What are we doing here?" Sabrina asked.

"We're investigating a crime, naturally," Mrs. Grimm said.

"Are you a police officer or something?" asked Daphne.

"Or something," the old woman said with a grin. "Why don't you get out and take a look around?" She walked away, apparently to snoop through the rubble.

Having a two-hundred-pound dog lie on her lap had given Sabrina a charley horse, so she and Daphne decided to get out and stretch their legs.

"She talks to the house, and cows, and has all these crazy rules. Now she thinks she's Sherlock Holmes," Sabrina muttered.

"Maybe it's a game," Daphne said. "I'm going to be a detective, too! I'm going to be Scooby Doo!"

Despite all of Sabrina's warnings, Daphne seemed to be having fun, something she hadn't had in nearly a year and a half. It was nice to see a smile on her sister's face and that old light in her eyes. It was the same look she used to have when their father would read them the Sunday comics or when their mother would let them invade her closet to play dress-up. Sabrina smiled and put her arm around the little girl's shoulders. She'd let her have her fun. Who knew how long it would last?

Just then, a long white limousine pulled into the clearing. It was bright and shiny with whitewall tires and a silver horse for a hood ornament. It parked next to Mrs. Grimm's car and a little man got out of the driver's side. He couldn't have been more than three feet high. In fact, he was no taller than Daphne. He had a big bulbous nose and a potbelly that the buttons of his black suit struggled to contain. But the most unusual thing about the man wasn't his size or his clothing. It was the pointy paper hat he wore on his head that read, I AM AN IDIOT. He rushed as quickly as he could to the other side of the car, opened the back passenger door, and was met with a barrage of insults from a man inside.

"Mr. Seven, sometime today!" the man bellowed in an English accent. "Do you think I want to sit in this muggy car all afternoon waiting for you to find time to open the door? You know, when you came to me for a job, I happily gave you one, but every day you make me regret it!"

A tall man in a purple suit exited the limousine and looked around. He had a strong jaw, deep blue eyes, and shiny black hair. He was probably the best-looking man Sabrina had ever seen, and her heart began to race. That was, until he opened his mouth again.

"What is this? Heads are going to roll, Mr. Seven," the man fumed as he looked around.

"Yes, sir," Mr. Seven answered.

"I was told that this was taken care of last night. It's just lucky that I realize that everyone who works for me is an incompetent boob or we would never have known this was still out here until it was too late. My goodness, look at that rubbish sitting there in broad daylight. What do the Three think I pay them for? I can't have this nonsense going on right now. Doesn't everyone realize that the ball is tomorrow? Heads are going to roll, Mr. Seven."

The little man nodded in agreement. His boss looked down at Sabrina and Daphne and scowled.

"Look, the tourists are already here and they're leaving their filthy children unsupervised. They are children, right, Mr. Seven? Not just a couple more of your kind?"

Mr. Seven's dunce cap had slid down over his eyes. He lifted it and gazed at the two girls. "They're children, sir."

"The way they are dressed you would think they were circus folk. You worked in the circus for some time, didn't you Mr. Seven?"

The little man nodded.

"Why, there ought to be a law about unsupervised children. This is a crime scene and it's crawling with kids. Mr. Seven, let's make that a law, if that isn't too much trouble?" the man continued.

"No trouble at all, sir," said Mr. Seven as he took a spiral-bound pad and a pen from his jacket pocket and furiously jotted down his boss's instructions.

"See how easy it is to be a team player, Mr. Seven? I like your change of attitude. If you keep this up we might be able to get rid of that hat," the man said.

"That would please me, sir."

"Let's not rush things, Mr. Seven. After all, you still haven't given these children my card, which is incredibly frustrating, especially since we discussed this just last night. What did I tell you, man?"

"Give everyone your card. It's good networking."

"Indeed it is," the man replied, tapping his toe impatiently.

"So sorry, Mr. Charming, sir," Mr. Seven said as he rushed to the girls and shoved a business card into each of their hands. It was purple with a golden crown on one side and the words MAYOR WILLIAM CHARMING—HERE TO LEAD YOU written on it in gold lettering. Underneath the name were a telephone number, an e-mail address, and a Web site: www.mayorcharming.com.

"Now, what was I saying before I had to tell you how to do your job, Mr. Seven?"

But before the little man could answer, Sabrina stepped forward. If there was one thing she couldn't stand, it was a bully.

"You were saying there ought to be a law against unsupervised children," Sabrina said angrily. "There should be a law against talking to people like they are morons, too!"

"Yes, that's correct. See, Seven, if this carnival girl can pay attention to the conversation, why can't you? Why, she can't be more than eight years old, and certainly slow in the head," Mayor Charming said.

"I'm almost twelve," Sabrina shouted. "And I'm not slow!"

Mayor Charming seemed startled by her anger.

"Where are your parents, child?" he snapped.

"We're here with our grandmother," Daphne answered. Sabrina spun around on her sister angrily. The old lunatic was not their grandmother.

"How splendid for you," Mayor Charming sneered. "And who is your grandmother?"

Daphne pointed to Mrs. Grimm, who was busy taking notes on a little pad of paper.

"Relda Grimm is your grandmother?" the mayor growled between gritted teeth. "When will this cursed family die out? You're like a swarm of cockroaches!"

Mrs. Grimm looked over, saw Mayor Charming, and quickly came to join them.

"Relda Grimm, I just met your granddaughters," the mayor said, as his face changed from a scowl to a smile. "They're the spitting image of their grandfather."

He bent over and pinched Daphne on the cheek. "Hopefully, they'll grow out of it," he muttered.

"Mayor Charming, what brings you all the way out here? I thought you'd be busy planning the fund-raiser. It's in a couple of days, correct?" said Mrs. Grimm with a forced smile.

"It is not a fund-raiser!" Charming insisted. "It's a *ball*! And it is tomorrow night. But you know how the community is. If I don't investigate every little stray cloud, the flock gets nervous. But then again, I could ask you the same question. What is the famous Relda Grimm doing in the middle of nowhere looking at a broken house?"

He was right—it was a house that had fallen down. Sabrina saw pieces of furniture and clothing sticking out of the pile and an old afghan quilt swinging from a stick in the breeze.

"I don't know what the farmer expected with such shoddy workmanship. He's lucky to have crawled out alive," he continued.

"So there was a survivor?" Mrs. Grimm said, writing in her notebook.

"Here she goes, Mr. Seven. You can almost see the wheels spinning in her head. Relda Grimm, private eye, out to solve the case that never was," the mayor said. "See, that's the problem with you Grimms. You could never quite grasp that in order to solve a mystery there must *be a mystery* to solve. A farmer built a flimsy house and it fell down. It was an accident. Case closed."

"Then why did you call it a crime scene?" Sabrina piped up.

Charming turned and gave her a look that could have burned a hole through her. "You must have misheard me, child," he said between gritted teeth. "Mr. Seven, take down this note, please. New law—children should not ask questions of their elders."

As the little man scribbled furiously in his notebook, Mrs. Grimm said, "We both know why we're here, Mayor."

Charming's face turned red. He tugged on his necktie and adjusted his collar. "This is *none of your concern*, Relda."

Before the old woman could respond, Mr. Canis joined the group.

"Well, if it isn't the big bad . . ."

"Mayor Charming!" said Mrs. Grimm angrily.

"Oh, I'm sorry, I heard you were going by *Canis* now." Charming grinned and leaned in close to Sabrina and Daphne. "Do yourselves a favor, girls, and check Granny's teeth before you give her a good-night kiss."

"Do you think it wise to provoke me?" Mr. Canis said as he took a step toward the mayor. Despite Mr. Canis's quiet demeanor, the words seemed to unnerve Charming.

"That's enough!" Mrs. Grimm demanded. Her voice shocked the girls, but the effect on the two grown men was even more startling. They backed away from each other like two school-boys who had been scolded by a teacher.

"The dog has found something," Mr. Canis said gruffly. He placed an enormous green leaf in Mrs. Grimm's hand and her eyes lit up in satisfaction.

"Well, look at that, Mayor Charming, I think we've found a clue. There might be a mystery to solve here, yet," she said, waving the leaf in the mayor's angry face.

"Congratulations! You found a leaf in the middle of all these trees," Charming scoffed. "I bet if you could bring out the forensics team you might find a twig, or even an acorn!"

"It looks a lot like a leaf from a beanstalk," the old woman replied.

Charming rolled his eyes. "That proves nothing."

"Maybe, maybe not, but it does seem odd that a fresh green leaf is out here in late November," Mrs. Grimm said. Sabrina looked around at the trees. Every limb was bare.

"Listen Relda, stop meddling in our affairs or you're going to regret it," said the mayor.

"If you don't want me meddling, then you must really do a better job of covering up your mistakes." Mrs. Grimm placed the leaf inside her handbag.

The mayor scoffed and then turned to Mr. Seven. "Get the door, you lumpy bag of foolishness!" he shouted. The little man nearly lost his paper hat as he rushed to the car door. Within moments, the limo was spitting gravel behind it as it drove away.

"Girls, why don't we take a walk over to that hill and sit by the tractor? I'd like to see this site from above," Mrs. Grimm said. Daphne took the old woman's hand and helped her up a sloped embankment where a lonely tractor was parked. When they reached the top, the old woman plopped on the ground and caught her breath. "Thank you, *liebling*. Either the hills are getting steeper or I'm getting older."

"Who was that man?" Daphne asked.

"Let's just say he's a royal pain," Mrs. Grimm replied. "Mr. Charming is the mayor of Ferryport Landing."

"What's with the bad attitude?" Sabrina said. The mayor reminded her of the orphanage's lunch lady, who seemed to delight in telling the children they were getting fat.

"He gets a little territorial sometimes."

"He and Mr. Canis sure don't like each other," Daphne added.

"They have a long history," the old woman said. She picked a small, black disk off the ground. "How interesting." She happily jotted down a note in her notebook. "A lens cap, from what looks like a very expensive video camera."

"Maybe it's just junk or something the farmer lost," Daphne said.

"Maybe, or maybe whoever is responsible for all that damage wanted a record." Mrs. Grimm tossed the lens cap into her handbag.

Just then, a white van with the words ACTION 4 NEWS painted on the side pulled up. The doors swung open and a cameraman and a pretty reporter in a business suit jumped out. The reporter checked her hair in a compact mirror as the cameraman handed her a microphone. They eyed the pile of lumber and brick and then spotted the girls and the old woman sitting on the hill. In no time, they were standing before them.

"Hello ladies, I'm Wilma Faye from Action Four News," the reporter said as she shoved her microphone in Mrs. Grimm's face. "We were wondering if you might be able to tell us what happened here."

"Oh dear, am I on television?" the old woman asked.

"You will be," the reporter replied. "Tell our audience what you witnessed."

"Oh, we didn't see anything, I'm afraid," said Ms. Grimm. "We only just got here."

The reporter groaned and the cameraman lowered his camera.

"This is just great!" Wilma Faye complained. "Five years of journalism school, graduating with honors and at the top of my class, and I'm out here in Ferryport Landing, in the cold, covering a house that collapsed."

"I'll get some shots of the damage," the cameraman said as he hoisted his heavy video camera back onto his shoulder and walked down the hill to the rubble.

"Good idea," the reporter replied. "Let's get out of here as soon as possible."

"Sorry I couldn't be of any help," said Mrs. Grimm.

"Oh, it's not your fault. I just keep getting sent out to this town when there isn't any news."

"Yes, unfortunately, there's not a lot of excitement in Ferryport Landing," the old woman agreed. Wilma Faye nodded and headed back to the van.

When the news crew had left, Mrs. Grimm removed the large green leaf and an odd little box covered in knobs and lights from her handbag. She placed the leaf on the ground, then pushed a red button on top of the box and waved it over the leaf.

"What are you doing?" Daphne asked.

"I'm analyzing it. Very scientific stuff," the old woman said just as the machine let out a loud honking sound that could only be described as a fart. "Just as I thought, it's from a giant beanstalk."

"There's no such thing as giant beanstalks." Daphne giggled.

Mrs. Grimm pointed at the clearing below. "What do you see?"

"A house that fell down?" the little girl suggested.

"Yes, but what else? What is surrounding the house?"

Sabrina focused her attention on the rubble. What was so unusual about it? Nothing, really, except maybe for the large area of sunken ground that surrounded it. "The earth is mashed around it," she said.

"And what could cause something like that to happen?"

"I don't know. What do you think?" Sabrina said, after running through the possibilities.

"I think a giant stepped on it," Mrs. Grimm answered. "Find a giant beanstalk leaf and you'll probably find a giant."

Daphne began to laugh but Sabrina was horrified. The old woman was getting crazier by the second.

"Well, I better go down and have a second look," the old woman said as she climbed to her feet. She walked back down the hill and joined Mr. Canis at the pile.

"She's funny." Daphne giggled.

Funny in the head, Sabrina thought.

"I want to ride on the tractor!" Daphne cried.

She jumped up and pulled her sister over to it. Sabrina lifted the little girl onto the seat, who then grabbed the wheel and turned it, making *vroom vroom* sounds as she pretended to drive.

"Look at me, I'm a farmer," she said in a goofy voice. Sabrina looked up at her sister and laughed. Daphne was the funniest person she had ever met.

"What kind of food do you grow on this here farm, Farmer Grimm?" the older girl played along.

"Why, I grow candy on this here farm." Daphne laughed. "Bushels and bushels of candy. Just sent my crop to market last week. Got me a pretty penny, I did."

Sabrina smiled, but then a shadow covered her heart. Why did the old lady have to lie about who she was? Why did she have to make up crazy stories? Why couldn't she be normal? Her house was warm and comfortable and as long as Sabrina kept an eye on Mr. Canis they might just be OK. If the old woman wasn't a lunatic she'd make a perfect grandmother.

"Sabrina, look at the house," Daphne whispered. She had stopped playing and was staring at the pile below.

Sabrina looked down at the clearing but saw nothing new.

"Do you see what I see?" Daphne cried, pointing.

"What? What do you see?"

"Come up here, you have to see it from up here."

Sabrina crawled up onto the tractor and stood high on its hood.

"Do you see it?"

And then Sabrina saw what her sister was so excited about and her heart leaped into her throat. The indentation surrounding the broken-down house had a shape.

"It's a footprint," she gasped.

3

Mrs. Grimm and Mr. Canis were pulling a prank on them. It explained why Mrs. Grimm talked to the house and served her crazy food and why Mr. Canis said so little and acted so weird. They were trying to make the girls look stupid, which made Sabrina furious. And worse, the joke didn't seem to end. They spent the rest of the day traipsing over the field for more "clues," until Mrs. Grimm looked at her wristwatch and said they'd better get home for dinner.

At the house, Mrs. Grimm prepared a huge plate of meatballs for the girls, complete with purple gravy, the recipe for which she claimed she'd gotten from a Tibetan monk. Too hungry to resist, Sabrina cut a meatball in half to make sure there weren't any poison pills inside and, finding none, took a bite. It tasted like pizza. She devoured the plateful and was working on seconds when Mrs. Grimm joined them, placing a weathered old book on the table.

"So, we've got a mystery on our hands, *lieblings*. We should do some research. A good detective always does her research. Let's see. Giants. What do we know about them? Oh, here's one, 'The Tailor and the Giant,'" she said as she flipped through the pages.

"OK, you've had your fun," Sabrina said fiercely. "Don't you think we're a little old to fall for your joke?"

Mrs. Grimm looked up from her book in astonishment.

"You can't really think it was a giant!" Sabrina cried.

"Well, of course I do," the old woman replied without blinking.

"Granny, there's no such thing as giants," Daphne said between bites of meatball.

"Oh dear, I knew your father wanted to distance himself, but I never imagined he wouldn't have at least taught you the basics," the old woman said. "No wonder you two have been looking at me like I'm crazy."

"What are you talking about?" Sabrina cried.

"I'm talking about this," Mrs. Grimm said as she flipped the book to its first page.

"*Grimms' Fairy Tales*," Daphne read aloud.

The old woman flipped to the next page. On it were portraits of two very ugly men. "Do you know who these men are?" she asked. The girls looked at the portraits but said nothing. They didn't look familiar to Sabrina. "These men were Jacob and Wilhelm Grimm, also known as the Brothers Grimm. Wilhelm was your great-great-great-great grandfather," said the old woman as she pointed to the portrait of a thin man with a large nose, tiny eyes, and long hair.

"*Grimms' Fairy Tales*! The fairy-tale guys?" Daphne cried.

"Yes, *liebling*, the fairy-tale guys. But there is nothing in this book that's a fairy tale. This is a history book. Every story is an account of something that *really* happened."

The girls looked at each other, unsure of what to say.

"Back when Jacob and Wilhelm were alive, fairy-tale creatures were still living among people," Mrs. Grimm continued. "You could still wake up and find a giant beanstalk on your farm or pixies in your barn or see a group of knights fight a dragon. But things were changing. For a long time, a tension had been building between humans and fairy-tale creatures. Everafters were being persecuted, even arrested or forced into hiding, just because they were different. Magic was banned and dragons were captured and caged. The brothers realized that the age of fairy tales might be coming to an end, so they set out to document as many stories as they could, for posterity's sake. Some of the things they wrote about in their book happened hundreds of years before they were born, while others Jacob and Wilhelm witnessed themselves. Naturally, as they collected these tales, they made a lot of friends of Everafters."

"What's an Everafter?" Daphne asked.

"That's what fairy-tale creatures call themselves. After all, *fairy-tale creature* implies that they are all some sort of monster or animal. Many of them are human, or once were, before a spell changed them. They can be quite touchy about it.

"So, like generations of poor and persecuted before them, many Everafters decided to move to America. Back then so much of this country hadn't been settled that for a group of folks trying to keep a low profile it seemed like the ideal place to live and thrive. Wilhelm acted as their ambassador. He found ships and used his connections to buy five square miles on the Hudson River. The Everafters built this town on the land, more Everafters came here from all over the world, and for a long time everyone lived together in peace. But inevitably human beings started to move into Ferryport Landing, and soon the Everafters felt endangered again. Wilhelm tried to convince everyone that there was nothing to worry about, but a small and vocal group of rebels argued that it was just a matter of time before they would be persecuted again. They saw humanity as an infestation that needed to be rooted out at the source, and began tormenting the humans who had once been their friends."

"That's not nice," Daphne said.

"I agree, but fear can make people do terrible things. Wilhelm tried everything he could but the rebels' popularity and numbers were growing. It wasn't long before a plan was discovered by Wilhelm to conquer Cold Spring—the next town over—and make it part of Ferryport's territory. Desperate to prevent what would surely be an all-out war between Everafters and humans, Wilhelm went to the most powerful witch in town, Baba Yaga. Together they cast a spell on the town, preventing any of the Everafters from leaving."

"And then what?" Daphne asked. Sabrina watched her sister's widening eyes. She seemed to believe every word the old woman had said, and even if she didn't really, the little girl was happy enough here to want to believe.

"Then the problems really began . . . especially for Wilhelm," the old woman said. "You see, to get Baba Yaga to cast such a powerful spell, Wilhelm had to sacrifice something of his own. Magic always has a price and what the old witch wanted was what Wilhelm had taken from the Everafters—his freedom. It's a price that hangs over our family to this day. A Grimm must stay in Ferryport Landing, just like the Everafters, as long as the spell is intact. It's the reason I couldn't come to the orphanage and get you myself."

"Isn't there something that could break the spell?" said Daphne.

"Yes, there is," Mrs. Grimm said as she shifted in her chair. "The spell will be broken when the last member of this family is dead. When there are no more Grimms, the Everafters will be free."

"What a bummer," Sabrina said.

"Indeed," Mrs. Grimm said, ignoring Sabrina's sarcasm. "But we make the best of it, and so do most of the Everafters. They keep a low profile, buying homes and starting businesses. Some have families and have even given up their magical powers and possessions in hopes of living more normal lives. And, with a couple of exceptions, things have been pretty peaceful in Ferryport Landing between humans and Everafters. But just a look through Jacob and Wilhelm's book, and the books of Hans Christian Andersen, Andrew Lang, Lewis Carroll, Jonathan Swift, and countless other chroniclers of Everafters shows you how fragile the peace is, and that trouble could be right around the corner. So, like Wilhelm, we have the responsibility of keeping this pot from boiling over. We watch the town, investigate anything strange or criminal, and document what we see, so that when we are gone our children will know what we went through. Think of us as detectives. Someday I will pass all of this on to you, as your Opa Basil passed it on to me when he died. It is your destiny. We are Grimms and this is what we do."

"But why didn't you pass it on to Dad?" Daphne wondered.

"Your grandfather lost his life because of our responsibilities," the old woman said as she lowered her eyes. "Henry wanted something else for his children, so when your mother became pregnant with you, Sabrina, they left Ferryport Landing. He wanted to protect you and give you normal lives. Even if it meant telling you I was dead."

"Don't talk about my mom and dad like you knew them!" Sabrina shouted. The rage inside her was bubbling over. "I've sat here and listened to your silly story, but you're not going to tell a fairy tale about my parents."

The old woman was startled and tried to stammer out an answer, but Sabrina wouldn't let her. She had Mrs. Grimm on the ropes and she wasn't going to let her up.

"You are not our grandmother!" the girl raged. "Our grandmother died before we were born! My dad told us so."

"Your dad lied to you, *liebling*. Henry tried to run from his destiny. He didn't want this life for you, but it is your destiny as well. Your being here is evidence enough that it is impossible to escape. You will see the truth soon enough, and when you do we will prepare you for what lies ahead."

"My father never told a lie in his life," Sabrina cried.

The old woman laughed as she got up from the table. "It sounds like he hid more from you than the family history. I'm sure you need some time to let this sink in, and I have some things I need from upstairs. We're going to the hospital to see the poor farmer who owned that house. He might be able to tell us more about what he saw."

She left the room and went up the stairs, where the girls could hear the jangling of keys and knew she was opening her secret room.

"That woman is a lunatic," Sabrina whispered.

"She is not!" Daphne cried. "What's a lunatic?"

"A crazy person. She thinks people live in the woods, she's nailed all the windows shut, she talks to the house, and now she thinks fairy tales and giants are real. We can't stay here."

"What if I don't want to go?"

"You don't get a say. Mom and Dad put me in charge when they weren't around, and you have to do what I tell you to do."

"You're not the boss of me." Daphne crossed her arms in front of her chest and huffed indignantly.

"We're out of here as soon as I see a chance," Sabrina declared.

• • •

After dinner, they were off to the hospital, with Mr. Canis driving again. Asking the old woman questions was pointless, as the car was as loud as ever. Once they had arrived at the hospital and Mr. Canis had turned off the engine, Mrs. Grimm said to the children, "OK, let's review what we know so far, so we don't get confused. It's important for detectives to review their clues."

The previous night was catching up with Sabrina. She was so tired she didn't even have the energy to argue.

"First, a farmhouse was destroyed by what appears to have been a giant's foot. A footprint surrounded the destruction," Mrs. Grimm continued. "Second, a giant beanstalk leaf was found at the scene, a definitive sign of a giant. And it has been touched by a giant."

"How do you know that?" Sabrina asked.

"Because Elvis smelled its scent on the leaf."

"How does Elvis know what a giant smells like?"

"Because," Mrs. Grimm said, pulling the brown fabric out of her handbag that she had held under the dog's nose that morning, "he smelled this. It's cloth from a giant's trousers. Take a sniff."

Daphne smelled the piece of cloth and looked as if she might be sick. "E-gad!"

"Everything has its own particular scent, but giants are really stinky," the old woman explained. "Everybody and everything they touch will stink like them, too. I knew Elvis's nose would help us find a clue."

"This is nonsense," Sabrina said with equal amounts of scorn and exhaustion.

Mrs. Grimm ignored Sabrina's protests. "Of course, there's also the lens cap from a video camera we found on the hill overlooking the farm. My guess is the criminal wanted to videotape the giant when he arrived. And lastly, Mayor Charming showed up and he's . . ."

"Is Mayor Charming Prince Charming?" Daphne asked.

"Why, yes, *liebling.*"

The little girl squealed in delight. "We met a celebrity!"

Mrs. Grimm chuckled, and then broke into a full laugh when she noticed the scowl on Mr. Canis's face.

"As I was saying, Mayor Charming showed up and tried to get us to give up our investigation," Mrs. Grimm continued. "If this were just an accident, he wouldn't have bothered to come by and check on it."

"When he first arrived, he was angry that someone he called *the Three* hadn't done a good job cleaning up the place," Daphne offered.

"*The Three* isn't a person, they're a coven of witches; Glinda the Good Witch of the North, Morgan Le Fay, and the gingerbread house witch, Frau Pfefferkuchenhaus. They work for the mayor. He calls them *magical advisors,* but they really just sweep whatever trouble there is under the carpet."

"I thought you said that Everafters gave up their magic," Sabrina said, hoping she had caught the old woman in a lie.

"No, I said some of them did, and in most cases, it was voluntary. I'm sure there's plenty of stuff hidden away in closets and attics all over Ferryport Landing," Mrs. Grimm replied. "Including, apparently, a magic bean I wasn't aware even existed. Let's go inside."

Ferryport Landing Memorial Hospital was tiny, at least small compared to the giant skyscraper hospitals Sabrina was familiar with in New York City. It had only two floors and no ambulances in front of the emergency room door. They left Mr. Canis in the car and, as they headed inside, passed a short, squat man and his two huge companions waiting by the hospital door. They were impeccably dressed in expensive suits, perfectly tailored to fit their extreme frames. The short man stared at Sabrina, sending a flash of heat to her face.

We look like idiots, Sabrina thought as she tried to tug her high-water pants down a little.

Inside, doctors and nurses rushed around the brightly lit hallways. The place smelled of cleaner and antiseptic, which tickled Sabrina's nose. The three Grimms managed to maneuver through the chaos and approach the information desk, where a portly receptionist sat talking on the phone. He had a large, round face and a toothy grin, and when he saw them, he put the phone to his chest and smiled.

"Can I help you ladies?"

"We're here to see Thomas Applebee. He was in an accident recently," Mrs. Grimm said.

"Oh, yes, the man whose house blew up. He's in room 222," the receptionist replied. "Popular fellow, he just had three people up to see him."

Mrs. Grimm cocked an eyebrow. "Indeed? Well, is there somewhere I should sign in?"

The receptionist handed the old woman a clipboard. Before she handed it back, she quickly pointed out three names on the list to the girls: a Mr. William Charming, a Mr. Seven, and a Ms. Glinda North had signed in ten minutes ago.

"Girls, we have to hurry."

They rushed down a hallway, through two double doors, and made a left, stopping at an elevator. Mrs. Grimm pushed the Up button several times.

"Why are we rushing?" Sabrina asked.

"Because Charming is here to erase the farmer's memory!" the old woman said as the elevator doors slid open and they stepped inside. They got out on the second floor, found room 222, and rushed inside.

On the bed was Thomas Applebee, a graying old man with his left arm in a sling and his right leg encased in plaster and held above the bed by a pulley system. Sabrina winced at how painful it looked and thought the poor man was lucky to be asleep. Standing over him were Mayor Charming, Mr. Seven (still wearing his insulting hat), and a rather chubby woman wearing a diamond tiara and a silver-and-gold dress. The woman was slowly emptying a bag of pink dust onto the sleeping patient. When she saw Mrs. Grimm, she dumped the contents all over the man and shoved the bag into her purse.

"Glinda, you've erased his memory," Mrs. Grimm cried. "I thought you were supposed to be a good witch."

The witch's face flushed red. She lowered her head and quickly made her way to the door.

"We all have to pay our bills, Relda," Glinda said as she walked out.

"Save your indignation," Charming added as he and Mr. Seven followed. "This is part of my job."

Mrs. Grimm looked discouraged. "He'll never be able to tell us anything," she said loudly, as if for the benefit of the three people who had just left. "And without an eyewitness account, we're never going to get to the bottom of this."

After several seconds, she poked her head out of the room. "They're gone."

"What are we doing here?" Sabrina asked. She didn't feel comfortable waiting around in the hospital room of a man she didn't even know. Especially after people had been dumping what looked like the contents of a vacuum cleaner bag all over him.

"We're waiting."

"For who?" Daphne asked, but no sooner had she said it than a thin, frail woman with gray-streaked black hair entered the room. When she saw Mrs. Grimm and the girls, she got a worried look on her face.

"Mrs. Applebee, I'm Relda Grimm and these are my granddaughters, Sabrina and Daphne. We heard about the accident. Are you OK?" Mrs. Grimm said.

"Oh, I'm fine. Thank you for asking. Do you know my husband?"

"Oh, no, we're just concerned citizens and neighbors. I happen to do a little detective work from time to time and I was thinking I might be able to help. How is your husband?"

Mrs. Applebee gazed down at the broken man and smiled sadly. "To be honest, I'm a little worried about him. He was raving earlier. The doctors gave him a sedative to calm him down . . . Wait a minute, he's waking up," she said as he began to stir. He opened his eyes and looked at the three strangers in his room.

"Thomas, how are you feeling?" Mrs. Applebee asked as she sat next to his bed and rubbed his hand.

"Debra, who are these people?" the farmer asked his wife.

"They're with the police," Mrs. Applebee replied.

Mrs. Grimm stepped forward. "Not the police, dear. I'm a detective . . . of sorts. Mr. Applebee, my name is Relda Grimm, and these are my granddaughters. I'm very glad to see you weren't too badly injured, considering . . ."

"You three are detectives?" Mr. Applebee looked from Mrs. Grimm to the children, eyeing them suspiciously.

"Yes," Mrs. Grimm said, causing Daphne to practically swell with pride.

"Well, I think a crime has been committed, Mrs. Grimm," Mr. Applebee said.

"You do?"

"They should arrest whoever dressed your granddaughters this morning."

"Thomas, stop it! I think they look adorable," Mrs. Applebee cried. "I'm sorry, he's been a grouch since we got here. He doesn't like hospitals."

Sabrina looked down at her goofy outfit and seethed with anger. *Who would buy a girl who was almost twelve a shirt with a monkey on it?*

"Well, what can I do for you, Mrs. Grimm?" Mr. Applebee grunted.

"Do you remember anything about the accident?" the old woman said.

"What accident?" the farmer asked.

Mrs. Grimm frowned.

"What accident!" Mrs. Applebee exclaimed. "Thomas, the house has been destroyed and I found you lying in the yard."

"I don't know what you're talking about. There's nothing wrong with the house," Mr. Applebee argued.

"Oh, dear, the painkillers are really doing a number on you," Mrs. Applebee said, shifting anxiously in her seat. The farmer returned his wife's stare with an innocent look.

"Mrs. Grimm, I don't think my husband is up to discussing the case right now," his wife said.

"I understand. Perhaps you might have a moment to spare us, then?"

"Of course." Mrs. Applebee gestured for them to follow her into the hallway.

"So sorry to trouble you," Mrs. Grimm said to the farmer as they walked toward the door. "I do hope you feel better soon, Mr. Applebee."

Daphne stopped and turned to the injured man. "I like my outfit," she said and stuck her tongue out.

Mr. Applebee stuck his tongue out, too, and the little girl stomped out of the room.

"He's acting very odd right now," Mrs. Applebee said when they were in the hallway. "I'm considering taking him out of this hospital."

"Oh, I'm sure he's in good hands. So, you said he was raving about something," Mrs. Grimm prompted.

"Oh, it's silly. He swore he'd seen a giant."

"Oh, well, wouldn't that be a sight." Mrs. Grimm chuckled.

"But I have a different theory about what happened," Mrs. Applebee explained. "There was a British man out to the farm several times, asking us if we would rent the place to him for a couple of nights. He said he needed the field for a special event, but only for a couple of days. At first he was very friendly, but when Thomas refused he got quite nasty."

"Has he come back?" Mrs. Grimm asked.

"Well, that's just it. A week later he did come back and apologized for being so rude. He said he wanted to make it up to us so he booked us into a fancy hotel in New York City, all expenses paid, and tickets to a Broadway show. We hadn't had a vacation in years—farming is a tough business—so I accepted."

"How nice. Did you enjoy your vacation?"

"Not at all. When I got there I found that the hotel didn't have any record of our reservation and the tickets to the show were counterfeit," Mrs. Applebee said angrily.

"You say *you* found out. Didn't your husband go with you?" Mrs. Grimm said.

"Oh, no, Thomas doesn't care for the city much," Mrs. Applebee sighed, tears forming in her eyes. "I took my sister. We had to use our own money for a hotel and the only place with a room was infested with bedbugs."

"How dreadful," Mrs. Grimm sympathized. "Mrs. Applebee, this man's name didn't happen to be Charming, did it?"

"Oh no, it was Englishman," the woman replied, sniffing.

"What did this Mr. Englishman look like?"

"I'm sorry, I never saw him. Thomas had all the dealings with him."

"One last question, Mrs. Applebee. I'm sure you want to get

back to your husband. Do either of you own a video camera?" Mrs. Grimm took a clean handkerchief out of her handbag and offered it to the woman. Sabrina noticed that a soft, pink powder fell from the handkerchief as the woman wiped her eyes.

"No, we don't. Mr. Applebee is a little tight with the money, if you know what I mean." Suddenly, Sabrina noticed a change in the woman's face. It seemed to wipe itself of all emotion and her eyes drifted into a blank stare.

"I'm sorry, have we met?" Mrs. Applebee asked, her voice distant.

"No," Mrs. Grimm replied. "But I hear you had a wonderful time in New York City."

"OK," Mrs. Applebee said. Then she turned and went into her husband's room without saying good-bye.

Mrs. Grimm pulled her notebook out of her handbag and jotted down some notes. "So, the plot thickens," she said with a wide smile. "We can definitely say there was a giant, now."

"There's no such thing as giants!" Sabrina said, a bit louder than she meant to. The declaration echoed down the hospital hallway.

"Sabrina!" Daphne shouted.

"You heard the woman," Sabrina said in a much lower tone. "This Mr. Englishman wanted to rent their farm for some special event. When the farmer wouldn't agree, he lost his temper and blew the place up. Charming is probably trying to cover this up because he's in on it."

"Sabrina, I'm proud of you," Mrs. Grimm said as she led them into the elevator. "You have incredible skills of deduction. You looked at the clues and chose the most likely path to solve the crime. You're going to make a great detective. But how do you explain the footprint?"

"Listen, I don't know where you live, but my sister and I are here on Earth where things can easily be explained without having to consider giants. Maybe whatever Englishman used to blow up the house caused the ground to sink."

"Brilliant, but there's a loose end in your theory. When someone blows something up, usually pieces fly everywhere. This house looked like it had been squashed from above," Mrs. Grimm pointed out. The elevator stopped and the Grimms stepped into the busy emergency room lobby.

"The house was stomped on," Daphne said.

"That's my theory," the old woman said as they left the hospital. "And I know who is responsible."

"Who is it?" Daphne squealed.

"I think you'll enjoy it more if it's a surprise."

"Well, hello, ladies," a voice said as three men emerged from the deep shadows that lined the pathway to the parking lot. They were the same men in suits who had been staring at them when they entered the hospital. The small, dumpy one held an iron bar that he kept smacking into his gloved hand. The men on either side of him stood like huge, muscle-bound bookends to their much shorter leader.

"Good evening, gentlemen," Mrs. Grimm said calmly, despite the fact that one glance told Sabrina the men were trouble.

"We hear you've been asking some questions about a certain piece of property," the dumpy leader said. Sabrina saw that his nose had been broken in three places. She could tell he wasn't a man to mess with.

"Then you've heard correctly, young man," Mrs. Grimm said as she placed herself squarely between the girls and the thugs. Daphne grabbed her sister's hand and squeezed tightly, but Sabrina hardly noticed. She was too awestruck by the old woman's courage.

"Well, if you know what's good for you, then you'll just forget about the whole thing," the leader said with a wicked grin that revealed the absence of a front tooth.

"If I knew what was good for me, I wouldn't be in this line of work," Mrs. Grimm replied. "Now, if you'd be so kind to let us pass, I really must get my granddaughters out of the cold air."

"In a minute, Relda." The leader grinned. "We just want to make sure you understand what we're trying to say."

"I seem to be at a disadvantage, young man. You know my name, but I don't know yours. Or better yet, who the unfortunate employer is who hired the likes of you three."

The two big men grunted angrily, but the leader raised his hands to quiet them. "No need to get rude, Relda. We're just having a conversation, ya know, trying to avoid a confrontation."

"Boys," Mrs. Grimm said with the tone of someone who has lost her patience. "I want you to go back to your boss and tell him that he should know it takes more than three thugs to make me give up. Now, good night."

She tried to pass the men, but as she did, the leader grabbed her jacket and pulled her close to his fat face.

"Some people can't take a hint."

Mrs. Grimm pulled a little silver whistle from around her neck and blew into it, but no sound could be heard. When she put it back inside her dress, the bullies laughed.

"I'm warning you. If you don't let us pass you are going to regret it," she said. Sabrina's heart began to pound. How could Mrs. Grimm be so calm? These men were about to tear her apart!

"Lady, it's *you* who's going to have the regrets."

eave my grandmother alone!" Daphne commanded. Before Sabrina could stop her, the little girl rushed forward and kicked the dumpy man in the shin. He cried out in pain and rubbed his leg. Mrs. Grimm then hit him on top of his head with her heavy, book-filled handbag. He crumpled to the ground and groaned. Seeing how easily their leader had fallen to a little girl and an old lady, the two other thugs laughed.

"What are you laughing at?" the leader snapped as he crawled to his feet.

"Sorry, Tony, we didn't mean to laugh," one of the goons said.

"What are you doing?" Tony bellowed.

"What?" the tall one asked defensively.

"You told her my name. We all agreed we were going to keep our identities secret."

The tall one shrugged. "Sorry, Tony, I didn't think."

"Steve, you just did it again," the other thug pointed out.

"You did it, too!" Tony shouted. "You just told them Steve's name."

"Who cares?" Steve said.

"Because they can identify us to the cops," Tony complained as he turned his attention back to Mrs. Grimm. He raised his heavy crowbar above his head and snarled. "Now we have to kill them!"

"Easier said than done," a voice said from behind them. Sabrina and Daphne turned to see Mr. Canis emerge from the shadows with Elvis close behind.

"Look out, here comes her boyfriend." Steve laughed. "You want to handle him, Bobby?"

"Shut up! Both of you!" Tony shouted. "Why don't you idiots just give them our addresses and phone numbers, too!"

"If you run off now, no one will get hurt," Canis offered. His voice was powerful and hard but the thugs just chuckled. Even Sabrina could tell that frail old Mr. Canis wasn't going to be able to stop them. Sometimes he looked as if his own clothes were too heavy for him to wear.

Sabrina realized now would be a great time to grab her sister and make their escape, but it didn't feel right. The old woman and her feeble friend needed their help. She would have to do something herself—find a weapon—a rock, a stick—anything she could use to fight the men off. But the pathway was as clean of debris as it was of people.

"Girls, get behind Elvis, please," Mr. Canis said, taking their hands and pulling them back so that the Great Dane was between them and trouble.

"Enough of this. Get him!" Tony ordered, and Bobby and Steve lunged at Mr. Canis. Sabrina was sure they had seen the last of the old man, but he caught both of the men by the throat, one in each hand, and lifted them off the ground, holding them aloft as their feet dangled and kicked. Even more shocking was the loud, guttural growl the old man released when he tossed the two thugs, sending them sprawling across the cold concrete ground. For ten yards they thumped and bounced, groaning with each painful smack against the pavement.

"All right, if that's the way you want to play it," Tony threatened as he pushed Mrs. Grimm roughly to the ground. He swung his iron bar wildly at Mr. Canis and rushed forward, but the old man quickly stepped sideways and tripped him, sending the thug to the pavement with his friends. Tony leaped up and rushed at Mr. Canis again, only to feel the same painful results.

"Hurry girls, we should get to safety," Mrs. Grimm said as she got up and led them away from the fight. Elvis trotted along beside them, barking warnings at the goons not to follow. When they got to the car, Daphne climbed in but anxiously peered out the windows. After several minutes, Mr. Canis had still not joined them.

"We shouldn't have left him. There were three of them, Granny! He can't fight them all," the little girl said, with tears running down her cheeks. Before Mrs. Grimm could calm her down, the car door opened and Mr. Canis crawled in behind the wheel. He was completely unharmed, and oddly, he had a little grin on his face.

"See, *lieblings*? He's just fine," the old woman said. She turned to Mr. Canis. "The girls were worried about you."

The old man turned in his seat and looked back at Sabrina and Daphne. He was his same painfully thin, watery-eyed old self. Daphne leaned forward and planted a kiss on his cheek. His face turned red with embarrassment.

"Don't you ever do that again!" she commanded as she hugged him tightly and then sat back into her seat. Mr. Canis nodded in agreement.

"I, for one, am thrilled at what's transpiring," Mrs. Grimm

said, taking out her notepad and pen. She began jotting notes frantically.

Sabrina was shocked. "Thrilled? We were almost killed."

"Killed? Oh Mr. Canis, doesn't she remind you of Basil?" Mrs. Grimm tittered.

Mr. Canis nodded.

"No, I think we have cause to celebrate," the old woman continued.

"Why, did you find a clue?" Daphne asked.

"No, not at all."

"Then, what's to celebrate?" Sabrina said.

"We're getting close, *lieblings*. When they send the goons, the bad guys are getting nervous."

"So what now?" Daphne asked.

"We'll follow those goons back to their hideout."

"What? Why would we do that?" Sabrina cried, remembering Tony and his crowbar.

"Because they're going to lead us right back to their boss. Ladies, we're going on a stakeout."

• • •

Mr. Canis managed to find the thugs' car in no time and he trailed them at a distance (which had to be pretty great, considering the noise coming from Mrs. Grimm's old rust bucket), driving high into the hills overlooking Ferryport Landing. They passed no other cars, just a few deer wandering by the road in the fading light. But Sabrina wasn't enjoying the scenery. She was a nervous wreck. She had already worried about Mrs. Grimm's sanity, based on the ridiculous fairy-tale story she had told earlier that day. Now the crazy old woman had them chasing three dangerous men. She wanted to kick herself for not escaping when they had had the chance, and decided that she and Daphne would make a run for it as soon as possible.

Eventually, the thugs' car pulled into the empty driveway of a small mountain cabin. Mr. Canis turned the engine and lights off and let the car coast along the road until they found a dense growth of trees to park behind. When they came to a stop, Mrs. Grimm opened up her handbag, fumbled through it, and took out a pair of odd-looking binoculars.

"What are those?" Daphne asked.

"They're binoculars for nighttime. They're called infrared goggles. I thought they might come in handy tonight," the old woman said as she handed them to Daphne. "Want to take a peek?"

Daphne took the goggles and raised them to her eyes.

"Oh, that's horrible!"

Sabrina looked out the window but saw nothing. "What? What do you see?" she asked nervously.

"You." The little girl giggled. "Here, take a look."

The older girl stuck out her tongue and took the goggles from her sister. When she looked through them, the darkness became illuminated in green light, and she saw the three thugs going into the cabin.

"Let's see who else turns up," Mrs. Grimm said. "Sabrina, would you mind letting Elvis out? He probably needs to stretch his legs."

Sabrina handed Mrs. Grimm the goggles and opened the door. Elvis lumbered out, causing the car to make noises that sounded like squeals of delight. With the door open, the girls could have easily made a break for it, using the woods for cover as they made their escape, but Daphne was leaning on the front seat asking questions.

"Granny Relda, are all the fairy tales true?"

"Almost all of them, but some are just bedtime stories to get kids to go to sleep. For instance, a dish never ran away with a spoon, and no cow that I know of has ever jumped over the moon."

"How about the three little pigs?"

Mr. Canis shifted in his seat but said nothing.

"Yes, dear, they are real," Mrs. Grimm replied.

"How about Snow White?"

"Yes, indeed. In fact, she's a teacher at Ferryport Landing Elementary. We're going to have to enroll you two there in a couple of weeks. She's very sweet and, as you know, very good with little people like yourself."

"What about Santa Claus?"

"I've never met him, but I have it on good faith that he is alive and well."

"I've got a question for you," Sabrina said. "These stories were written hundreds of years ago. How could all these people still be alive?"

"Easy child, it's magic," Mrs. Grimm explained.

"Duh!" Daphne said to her sister, as if it were common knowledge.

Sabrina shot her an angry look, but the little girl ignored it.

"Granny Relda, have you ever seen a giant?" Daphne asked.

"Of course, *liebling*, I've even been to the giant kingdom on a couple of occasions. The last time I was nearly squished by the Giant Queen's toe." Mrs. Grimm laughed. "As an apology, she gave me that piece of fabric."

"Well, if there really are giants, how come we haven't seen any yet?" Daphne asked.

"There weren't any around until yesterday," Mrs. Grimm said. "Long ago, the Everafters realized that giants were just too unpredictable. They caused as much destruction when they were happy as they did when they were mad, and once they planted themselves somewhere it was impossible to move them. Imagine trying to plant seeds on your farm with a sleepy giant lying across it! When humans started moving into Ferryport Landing, everyone realized that giants were just too big to disguise. Of course, the giants didn't agree and refused to go back to their kingdom. Your great uncle Edwin and your great aunt Matilda tricked them into climbing their beanstalks, and once they were all up there, the townsfolk chopped the beanstalks down."

"What good would that do?" Daphne asked.

"No beanstalk—no way into our world. Of course, there were a couple of people who didn't much care for the plan. In the old days, people would plant magic beans and climb up the beanstalks just to steal the giants' treasures. Lots of people were foolish enough to try, but only one ever survived the ordeal," Mrs. Grimm said.

"Jack?" Daphne asked.

"You are correct, *liebling*. Jack robbed many giants and killed quite a number of them, too. In his day he was very rich and famous, though I hear he's working at a Big and Tall clothing store downtown, now. I can't imagine he'd be too happy doing that."

"Are you going to sit here and tell us that Jack was a real person?" Sabrina snapped.

"Was and is, my love," Mrs. Grimm replied.

"So, let's just say all this is true. If all the beanstalks were destroyed, how did a giant get down here?" Sabrina asked, confident that she had tripped up the old woman.

"Ah, *liebling*, that is indeed the mystery we are trying to solve. Whoever did it had to have a magic bean, and I thought we had accounted for all of them. It would help if we knew why they wanted to let a giant loose."

"I'll bet he was a big one, Granny Relda. Probably a thousand feet high!" Daphne exclaimed.

"Oh, sweetheart, he's probably no bigger than two hundred feet tall," Mrs. Grimm said.

Sabrina looked at her little sister in the moonlight and frowned. Daphne's eyes were as big as Frisbees. Sabrina was losing her little sister to the old lunatic. For a year and a half it had been just the two of them, and Sabrina had done everything she could to keep them together and safe. She had protected her sister from nasty Ms. Smirt, the horrible kids in the orphanage, and all those foster parents, and now she was unable to protect her from a crazy old woman.

Just then, Elvis let out a low growl.

"Someone's coming," Mrs. Grimm warned as headlights flashed behind them. "Everyone get down."

They all huddled under the windows as a car passed by and headed toward the cabin. When it was far enough away, they lifted their heads.

"I don't think he saw us," Daphne said.

The old woman lifted the goggles to her eyes.

"Well, Sabrina, we've got more evidence for your theory. That's Mayor Charming's car," Mrs. Grimm said. "I didn't expect to see him here."

Mr. Canis rolled his window down and sniffed the cool mountain air. Then, as if he had smelled something foul, his nose curled up. The odd thing was that Elvis, who was sitting outside of Mr. Canis's window, had the same expression. The two of them were smelling something they didn't like.

"Charming is knocking on the door," Mrs. Grimm reported.

Mr. Canis turned in his seat. "Child, open your door. The dog should get back into the car."

Daphne opened her door and called for Elvis, but the Great

Dane stood motionless, sniffing the air as if he was dedicating all his attention to it.

"They're talking," the old woman continued, still looking through her goggles.

"Get into the car, dog," Mr. Canis called sternly. Elvis turned to face him but kept sniffing.

"Wait a minute, Charming is running to his car. Something has got him spooked," Mrs. Grimm remarked. "And you won't believe who's with him!"

It was the perfect opportunity. The old woman was watching the house and Mr. Canis was distracted by Elvis. Sabrina grabbed her sister's hand, opened her car door, and pulled Daphne out.

"What are you doing?" Daphne cried.

"We're getting out of here this minute!" Sabrina replied, but before they could even take a step Elvis blocked their escape with his huge body.

"Come on, you big flea hotel. Get out of the way!" Sabrina shouted, but the dog refused to budge.

"Don't call him a flea hotel!" Daphne scolded. "He's sensitive!"

Elvis let out a horrible whine. It was followed by an earth-shaking thump that sent the girls tumbling to the ground.

"What was that?" Sabrina asked, trying to stand up.

"Girls, get into the car," Mr. Canis urged. His face looked serious and dark.

"We're not going anywhere with you," Sabrina cried as she got to her feet.

"*Lieblings*, please. Something is coming," Mrs. Grimm begged.

"Something is coming? What does that mean? Enough with the stories, OK?" Sabrina yelled. "You're just trying to scare us and give my sister nightmares so that maybe we'll be too frightened to leave you." It was almost as if the mini-earthquake had knocked something loose inside of Sabrina, an anger and frustration at being abandoned, drifting from foster home to foster home, always hoping for someplace where they could be happy, but finding that whenever they got close, it was tainted with some sort of craziness.

"Sabrina, we can discuss this at another time. Please get into the car," Mrs. Grimm pleaded once more.

"I don't want to hear another word about fairies and goblins and giants or Jack and the Beanstalk or Humpty Dumpty!" Sabrina raged as Elvis let out a shrieking howl. "I know the difference between reality and a fairy tale!"

But she had hardly finished her rant when something fell out of the sky. It was monstrous and encircled the car and lifted it off the ground. Sabrina couldn't believe what she was seeing, but it was there, right in front of her.

It was a hand—a giant hand.

Her eyes traveled up the arm, higher and higher, until she found a giant head and then immediately wished she hadn't. Boils as big as birthday cakes pocked the giant's greasy skin. A broken nose zigzagged across his face, and one dead white eye seeped puss while the other one was lined with the crust of sleep. Hairs as thick as tree trunks jutted out of his nose and hung over a mouthful of broken, misplaced, yellow-and-green teeth. He wore the hides of dozens of gigantic animals, including the head of what looked like a giant bear for a helmet. The dead bear's sharp fangs dug into his bald head, threatening to pierce his brain. His boots were made from more hides, and tangled in the laces were several unfortunate saplings.

The giant lifted the car up to his repugnant face and looked inside like a child inspecting a toy. With his free hand he picked his nose.

"Where is Englishman?" he bellowed. "Why does he hide from me?"

Sabrina couldn't see what was going on in the car as it was nearly two hundred feet off the ground. Were Mrs. Grimm and Mr. Canis even still alive? It was all so horrible that the two girls barely noticed that something had dropped from the car, landing with a clang at their feet.

"You cannot hide from me, Englishman!" the giant shouted as he lifted his enormous leg and stomped down hard on the little mountain cabin, flattening it like a pancake. Pieces of timber and stone sprayed into the air, just missing the girls. Sabrina and Daphne gasped. The three thugs—Tony, Steve, and Bobby—had been inside the cabin. There was no way any of them could have escaped.

Looking down at the destruction, the giant let out a sickening laugh. He stuffed the car into a greasy shirt pocket, lifted his other humongous leg, and walked away, carrying the remains of the mountain cabin in the treads of his boots. The earth shook violently and a ripple spilled across the land as if someone had tossed a stone into a pond to see it skip. Because of his mammoth stride, the giant completely disappeared over the horizon after just a dozen steps. Only the distant rumbling of his disastrous footfalls and the angry growls of Elvis remained.

The girls stood completely frozen. Competing with Sabrina's fear was another unsettling emotion—humiliation. Mrs. Grimm had been telling the truth the whole time and Sabrina had refused to listen. Sabrina had deliberately been a jerk to the old woman, and now she might never see her again to tell her she was sorry. She moved to comfort her sister, but Daphne pulled away. The little girl rushed over to pick up whatever had fallen from the car. It was Mrs. Grimm's handbag.

"She was telling the truth and you have been a big snot since the first minute. Tell me now if you think she's crazy," Daphne said furiously.

"I don't think she's crazy," her older sister said, but Daphne had already turned and was marching down the road. "Where are you going?"

"I'm going to rescue our family," the little girl called back without stopping.

abrina looked down the long empty road. They had been walking for over an hour, and not so much as a bicycle had passed them. If they didn't get a ride back to the house soon, the girls would be walking all night.

The time might have passed more quickly if there had been a little conversation, but for an hour, Daphne had marched ahead of Sabrina, refusing to speak. Even Elvis, who followed closely behind, was ignoring her, but since he was a dog, his silence was a lot easier to take. But Daphne hadn't been quiet for longer than five minutes since she was born. She was even a noisy sleeper.

"How was I supposed to know?" Sabrina cried. "Anybody would have thought she was crazy!"

"I didn't," Daphne said, finally breaking her silence.

"You don't count. You believe everything," Sabrina argued.

"And you don't believe in anything," the little girl snapped. "Why are we even talking? You don't care what I think, anyway."

"That's not true!" Sabrina said, but before the words had left her mouth she knew they were a lie. What Daphne thought hadn't mattered in a long, long time, at least not since their parents had deserted them. But it wasn't like Sabrina wanted it that way. She was only eleven and didn't want to have to make all the decisions for both of them. She would love to feel like a kid and not have to worry about whether they were safe. But that wasn't how things were. Unfortunately, she realized now, she had never considered what Daphne thought when it came to their best interests.

"Whatever!" Daphne muttered, and continued her angry march back to the house.

Elvis followed, sniffing the air wildly for the giant's stench. Sabrina could see that he took his guard dog duties seriously. Every little buzz and cracking sound had to be investigated. The dog darted back and forth, peering through the barbed-wire fence that separated the road from the endless forest. Once he was confident that the swaying limbs of the pines or the occasional rooting woodchuck were not a giant sneaking up on them, he trotted to the center of the road and put his huge nose back to work.

"This is ridiculous. We'll never get home if we walk," Sabrina said. Her feet were aching, and at the pace they were going they'd be lucky if they made it back to the house by nightfall the next day.

"You're not helping!" Daphne cried as she spun around. Her face was red and she had her hands on her hips.

"What do you want me to do?" Sabrina asked. "The old woman . . ."

"Our grandma," Daphne corrected.

"Whoever she is . . . just got carried off by a giant and we are trapped in the middle of nowhere. I'm sorry, but I've run out of ideas!"

Daphne's shoulders loosened and her expression sank. She walked over to a fallen tree trunk next to the road, sat down, and began to cry. Elvis trotted over and nuzzled her, licking the little girl's tears from her chubby cheeks, and adding his whines to her sobbing. Sabrina sat down beside her sister and put her arm around the little girl.

"You don't care if we ever find them," Daphne sniffled, pulling away. "Now you can run off like you planned with no one to stop you."

Sabrina thought for a moment before she responded. She had to admit to herself that running away was her first instinct.

"Daphne, that monster was real. We can't fight that by ourselves. Even if we knew where he carried them off to, I don't think we could get them back. What are a seven-year-old and an eleven-year-old going to do about a giant?"

"You're almost twelve," Daphne said, wiping her eyes on the sleeve of her fuzzy orange shirt. "Besides, you heard Granny Relda. We're Grimms and this is what Grimms do. We take care of fairy-tale problems. We'll find a way to save Granny and Mr. Canis."

"How?"

"With this," Daphne said, holding the old woman's handbag above her head.

Sabrina took it from her sister and fumbled through it. Inside were Mrs. Grimm's key ring, the swatch of fabric the old woman had said came from a giant, books, her notebook, and a small photograph. Sabrina pulled it out.

"Mom and Dad," she said, as surprise raced through her. It was a picture of their parents, young and in love. Their dad had his hand on their mother's very pregnant stomach and they were both grinning. Granny Relda stood next to them, beaming, while Mr. Canis was off to the side, stone-faced as ever.

It had been more than a year and a half since Sabrina had seen a picture of her parents. The police had seized everything during the investigation and promised that when it was over they'd get everything back. But when the cops gave up looking for her mom and dad, their promises faded away. Now Sabrina's bitterness toward her parents faded, too. She held the snapshot as if it was a delicate treasure. It was evidence that her parents had existed, that at one time she and her sister had been part of a family. And it was obvious, seeing Granny Relda and her father standing side by side, where her father had gotten his warm round face. She glanced at Daphne and saw that face in her sister, as well. She looked at her father's blond hair and recognized her own. Daphne had her mother's jet-black hair; Sabrina had her high cheekbones and bright eyes. How could her mom and dad have walked away from their family? Proof that they should be together was right there in their faces.

Daphne hovered over her sister to get a better view, tears still running down her cheeks. Sabrina turned the picture over. Someone had written, "The Family Grimm—Relda, Henry, Veronica, Mr. Canis, and the soon-to-be-born baby, Sabrina."

"Why did he lie to us about her?" Sabrina whispered as she tucked the family portrait safely into her pants pocket.

"I don't know," Daphne answered quietly.

"And what happens if we start to love her and she abandons us, too?" the older girl asked, trying to hide the hurt in her voice.

"Maybe she won't," Daphne said. "Maybe she'll just love us back."

The little girl wiped her eyes and dug into Granny Relda's handbag. She pulled out their grandmother's giant key ring. "She wanted us to have these keys. She wants us to go home."

If we can even get home, Sabrina said to herself as a light caught the corner of her eye. She looked down the road. There were headlights approaching.

The two girls got up from the log and brushed themselves off.

"What should we do, stick out our thumbs?" Daphne asked.

Sabrina didn't know. They'd never hitchhiked before. In the past, whenever the girls had found themselves alone or on the run, they slipped under the turnstiles in the subway stations and traveled New York City's subterranean highway.

Sabrina stuck out her thumb and Daphne did the same. The car came to a screeching stop. It sat still for a moment, with its engine humming, blinding the girls with its high-beam lights so that they had to shield their eyes with their hands.

"Well, that was easy," Daphne said. "What's he doing?"

"I don't know," Sabrina said, stepping to the side. "Maybe he doesn't want to give us a ride."

Suddenly, the car let out a long, eardrum-rattling honk, followed by more engine revving. To Sabrina, it seemed as if the car were an animal, waiting for the right time to pounce on them. She recalled hearing stories about hitchhikers being killed by lunatics. Hitchhiking didn't seem like such a great idea anymore. She grabbed her sister's hand and pulled her off the road. As if in response, the car revved its engines again.

"Run!" Sabrina cried. Surprised, Daphne stumbled along beside her but did what she was told. The two of them raced back the way they had come, hand in hand. Elvis followed closely behind, turning his big head to bark out the occasional angry warning at the menacing car, but it had little effect on whomever was behind the wheel. The squeal of tires on asphalt told Sabrina that they were now being chased. The car honked again, sending a shocking jolt through her bones, and then suddenly it veered to the other side of the road. It sped up and passed the girls, then spun around, leaving black stains on the asphalt and the smell of burning rubber in Sabrina's nose. It was a police car, now stretched across the road, blocking the girls' escape.

The door opened and a short, stout, pear-shaped man stepped out. He wore a beige police uniform with shiny black boots, a billy club at his utility belt, and a wide-brimmed hat that fastened under his three chins. His face was puffy and pink with a nose that angled slightly upward, so that a person could see up his nostrils. On his shirt was a shiny, tin star that read FERRYPORT LANDING SPECIAL FORCES and a name tag underneath it that said SHERIFF HAMSTEAD.

"Girls, why are you running?" the sheriff asked in an unusually high-pitched voice that sent shivers into Sabrina's belly.

"We thought you were trying to kill us," Daphne said angrily. Sabrina flashed her a look, letting her know that she would do the talking.

"I see. Well, I'm sorry if I gave you two a start, but it's not safe for little girls like yourselves to be walking out here in the dark. These roads can be treacherous," the sheriff said.

"Treacherous?" Daphne asked.

"Dangerous," Sabrina explained.

"I got a call that you were out here, so I came looking," the portly man continued as he hoisted his sinking pants up around his waist. "Why don't you two hop into the squad car and I'll take you home?" He pointed to Elvis. "I don't know if we can put your horse in there, but we'll try."

"He's not a horse," Daphne said. Then, realizing the sheriff was joking, she added, "You can't tease him. He's very sensitive."

Hamstead leaned down and scratched Elvis under the chin. "Oh, I'm sure he is, aren't you, Elvis?"

The big dog growled and snapped at the sheriff's hand.

Hamstead pulled it away just in time, but then rubbed it with his other hand as if the dog had gotten a lucky bite.

"How do you know Elvis?" Sabrina said suspiciously.

"Oh, Elvis and I have met before. You must be Relda Grimm's grandchildren. I heard you were in town," the man said. "I'm the local sheriff, Ernest Hamstead."

"I'm Daphne," the little girl offered.

"Sabrina," Sabrina muttered.

"So, do you two need a ride home or are you trying to raise a million dollars for the March of Dimes?"

Sabrina nodded and Hamstead opened the squad car's backdoor. Elvis clumsily climbed in and the sheriff shut the door behind him. Sabrina and Daphne walked around the car and got in on the passenger's side of the front seat.

Sheriff Hamstead squeezed and shifted his way into the car, breathing heavily as if carrying a great burden. He had left the keys in the ignition (Sabrina guessed so that he wouldn't have to fish them out of his tight pants), so as soon as he was settled, he started up the squad car and headed in the direction of Granny's house.

"So, I assume you two have already concocted some elaborate scheme to get your granny and her friend back?" Hamstead asked. The girls looked at each other, unsure of what to say.

"So you know about this?" Sabrina asked, dumbfounded.

"Yep," Sheriff Hamstead said. "Hard to miss a two-hundred-foot giant carrying grandmas away into the night, don't you think? I don't want you two girls to worry. Your granny is a tough cracker. I've seen her in bigger jams than this one and besides, she's got the entire Ferryport Landing Special Forces Squad working on the case. I know you two have been trained for this kind of thing, but we like to take care of our own problems here in Ferryport Landing."

Daphne cupped her hand around Sabrina's ear. "Have we been trained?" she whispered.

"I don't know what he's talking about," Sabrina whispered back.

"Are you an Everafter?" the little girl said, returning her attention to the sheriff.

The sheriff looked over and winked a yes at Daphne. She squealed in delight. "Which one?"

Suddenly, the squad car's CB radio crackled to life. "Hamstead? Sheriff Hamstead?" a man's voice fumed. It sounded oddly familiar to Sabrina.

The sheriff seemed nervous. When he tried to pick up the handset, it fumbled in his sweaty hand before he finally got ahold of it.

"I'm here, boss. En route now," Hamstead said.

"That's fantastic news, Hamstead. Nice to know you can do something that's asked of you. If you care at all, I picked up our little troublemaker about a half an hour ago and he's sitting in a cell as we speak. So all I'm asking from you is to get those little trolls back to the mansion, ASAP! I can't have any headaches ruining tomorrow's festivities."

Sabrina's heart froze and as she looked at her sister, she saw the same horror reflected in Daphne's eyes. The voice on the police radio was Mayor Charming's! The car had come to a stop sign, and Sabrina knew they had to act.

"Daphne, do you remember that time Mr. and Mrs. Donovan took us to that three-day lima bean cook-off festival?" Sabrina asked casually, hoping the girl would remember the crazy foster couple they had lived with for three weeks the previous year. The little girl grimaced, obviously remembering the pickled lima bean pie Mrs. Donovan was so proud of, but then a light in her eyes told Sabrina she also remembered their daring escape. Sabrina slipped her hand into her sister's and quickly pulled on the door handle. Before Hamstead could react, the girls were out of the car and freeing Elvis from the backseat.

"Hey!"

The sisters ran to the side of the road where a five-foot barbed-wire fence lined the edge of the forest. There was no way to climb it; the barbed wire's sharp teeth would tear them apart. Their only chance was to try to scurry between the rusty wires to the other side. Desperate, Sabrina stood on one of the wires, reached down and grabbed a safe spot on the next highest one, and pulled upward as hard as she could, creating a hole her sister could crawl through.

"Go!" Sabrina shouted, carefully watching the portly sheriff struggling out of the car. Daphne scampered through the small gap to the other side. The little girl got to her feet and tried to mimic the trick she had just seen Sabrina do. The result was a small gap Sabrina couldn't possibly fit through.

"It's heavy," Sabrina coached Daphne, "you have to be strong."

"I am!" the little girl cried, pulling harder.

"Girls, you can't run!" Hamstead shouted angrily, as he finally freed himself from the car. Elvis positioned himself between Sabrina and the sheriff and barked a warning when the man took a step forward.

Sabrina got down on her hands and knees and tried to crawl through, but before she could get to the other side, Hamstead, dodging Elvis, was on top of her, grabbing her legs and trying to pull her back out.

"You're coming with me!" he squealed.

Sabrina kicked wildly and looked back into the sheriff's face, and what she saw bewildered her. Sheriff Hamstead was going through a disturbing metamorphosis. His already pug nose became a slimy pink snout. His round face puffed up to three times its size, and his ears turned pink and pointy and migrated to the top of his head. His chubby fingers melded into thick black hoofs, and his back bent over until he was literally on all fours. Hamstead had turned into a pig—an angry, determined pig in a policeman's uniform.

"I can't hold it any longer," Daphne cried, wide-eyed at what she was witnessing. Sabrina kicked one more time and felt her foot sink into Hamstead's gelatinous belly. His piggy face turned white and he fell onto his back, honking and gasping for air as his little legs flailed back and forth. Just as suddenly as he had changed to a pig, he changed back to a man.

Daphne's arms gave out and the barbed wire came down on top of Sabrina, snagging her pants. Daphne vainly tried to lift it again, but the taut wire barely moved.

"What are we going to do?" Daphne cried as Hamstead staggered to his feet. He rushed toward Sabrina, this time as a full man. Suddenly, Sabrina heard a series of notes, as if someone in the woods was playing a flute, followed by a buzzing sound that grew closer and closer. Sabrina peered through the trees nervously, remembering the music from the night before.

"They're coming, aren't they?" Daphne said, and before she finished the question a cloud of little lights zipped out of the forest and surrounded them. This time the lights didn't attack. Instead, they hovered as if waiting for instructions. Another note pierced the night air and the little lights buzzed into action, perching on the barbed wires that had Sabrina caught and, with a flutter of wings, pushing at the lowest wire and pulling the other one up, creating a hole big enough for Sabrina to scamper through. When she got to the other side, the little lights let go of the wires.

Hamstead, trapped on the other side of the fence, squealed in frustration and searched for an opening. He waddled back and forth, huffing and grunting, but found nothing that would allow his human or pig form to pass. Desperately, he got to his hands and knees and tried to squeeze through the wires. And that's when Elvis made his move. The big dog ran full steam right at Hamstead like some kind of fur-covered locomotive. He leaped onto Sheriff Hamstead's broad back and used it as a springboard. The sheriff let out a painful grunt as Elvis sailed effortlessly over the top of the fence and landed on all fours.

The chubby policeman quickly recovered. He stood up,

grabbed a fence post, and began to climb. Sabrina knew she had to do something. She grabbed another post and pushed all her weight against it. Discovering it was quite loose in the ground, she shook it back and forth as hard as she could, and the fence swayed uncontrollably.

"Hey, stop that!" Hamstead shouted nervously as he clung to the fence.

Daphne rushed to Sabrina's side and together they shook the fence even harder. Suddenly, with a loud tearing of fabric, Sheriff Hamstead's body thumped to the ground on his side of the fence. He groaned and let out an angry cry. After a moment, he picked himself up. Unfortunately, his pants had not survived the fall. They hung from the sharp teeth of the barbed-wire fence, leaving the sheriff in just a pair of droopy long johns. Defeated, he hobbled back to his car.

"He's leaving," Sabrina said as she followed her sister into the dark woods.

"He turned into a pig," Daphne whispered.

"I saw him," Sabrina replied. "But I think we have another problem."

The little lights waited patiently ahead of them. They darted into the woods and then came back out, as if they wanted the girls to follow them.

"What do you want?" Sabrina asked, and the lights shimmered and blinked an answer.

"Should we follow them?" said Daphne.

"I don't see that we've got much of a choice," Sabrina said, thinking the lights might attack if they didn't.

She took her sister's hand and they walked through the dark woods, with Elvis trotting closely behind. Low-hanging branches blocked their path, and with each step the girls had to dodge and weave to get through. Several times Sabrina walked into trees, feeling the prickly spindles of a pine or the crusty bark of an oak tear at her clothes and skin. The lights guided them, slowing down occasionally to see if they were keeping up.

"They're making sure we're following them," Sabrina said, wondering if it was a good thing or a bad thing. Soon, the girls stepped into a clearing. In the center was a pile of junk. An old refrigerator, a couple of burned-out microwaves, some abandoned teddy bears, and a broken toilet had been assembled into a massive chair. Sitting on the junk "throne" was a boy with a mop of blond hair that was tussled and dirty. He wore a pair of baggy blue jeans and a green hooded sweatshirt in desperate need of a washing, and in his hand he held a small sword. But most interesting was the golden crown that rested on his head.

"Pixies," he called to the little lights. "What have you found?"

The little lights erupted into a loud buzzing.

"Spies, you say?" the boy asked. "Well, what do we do with spies?"

There was more buzzing in response, and a wicked grin appeared on the boy's face.

"That's correct." He laughed. "We drown them!"

6

hen the girls protested their kidnapping, the army of pixies surrounded them and delivered several stings. Nursing their wounds, the girls were forced to follow the odd boy farther into the woods.

"Where are you taking us?" Sabrina asked, but the boy just laughed.

Soon, they came to the end of the forest, where a tall fence blocked their way. Built into the fence was a door, and the boy pushed it open. The girls stepped through and found themselves standing in front of a tarp-covered swimming pool in the backyard of a two-story suburban-style house. Some pixies swirled around the tarp and lifted it off the pool, while others zipped off and returned with a rope. They stung

Sabrina's arms relentlessly until she put them behind her back, and then they tied the rope around her wrists.

The boy stuck the tip of his sword into Sabrina's back. He forced her onto the diving board. "You've made a terrible mistake, spy!" he shouted.

"We're not spies!" Sabrina exclaimed.

"Tell it to the fish!" the boy hollered, causing the little lights to make a tittering noise that sounded like laughter. Sabrina looked down at the pool and wondered how deep the water was. There was a diving board, so it had to be deep, and with her arms tied behind her she'd certainly drown if the icy water didn't freeze her to death first. She tugged at the ropes, but each pull just tightened them around her wrists.

"So, spy, would you like to repent your crimes before you meet your watery doom?" the boy asked.

"What crimes?" Sabrina cried, and then took a deep breath, certain he would push her in. But after several moments, nothing happened.

"The crime of trying to steal the old lady away from me," the mop-topped boy declared.

"Granny?" Daphne asked from the side of the pool.

"The one they call Relda Grimm."

"Relda Grimm is our *grandmother* and we're not trying to steal her. We're trying to save her!" Sabrina shouted.

"Save her?" the boy asked suspiciously. "Save her from what?"

"A giant," the two girls called out together.

Sabrina could sense their captor's confusion. She turned and found him talking to several of the little lights that hovered around his head.

"Well, of course it makes a difference," the boy replied, annoyed.

"We're trying to get home. We need to save her before it's too late," Daphne pleaded.

The boy groaned and quickly untied Sabrina's wrists. "Where did this happen?" he asked. "How big was the giant?"

But Sabrina didn't answer. Instead, she spun around, grabbed the boy by the shoulders, and heaved him into the pool, sending a splash of water and soggy dead leaves high into the air. The sword had slipped from the boy's hand as he fell, and with nimble fingers, Sabrina caught it. She leaped to safety on the side of the pool and waved the sword threateningly at the pixies.

"You're going to let us walk out of here," she demanded. There was no movement at first, but then they flew around the pool, making a laughing sound, as if they were chuckling at their leader's misfortune. Sabrina stood dumbfounded, unsure of what to do next.

A geyser of water shot high into the air, with the soaked boy riding its crest. When the water crashed back into the pool, the boy stayed aloft, several feet above Sabrina. Two huge wings had come out of his back and were flapping loudly. Oddly enough, the boy was laughing.

"You think this is funny?" Sabrina exploded. She began making jabs at the boy, who flew effortlessly away from her thrusts. "A kid and a bunch of flying cockroaches kidnapping girls and threatening to kill them? That's how you losers have fun?"

"Aww, we wouldn't have killed you. We were just fooling," the boy said.

"Well, if you're finished with your stupid, psychotic games, my sister and I have to rescue our grandmother," Sabrina declared. She took Daphne's hand and turned to leave. Elvis joined them, but Sabrina shot him an angry look. The dog had spent the entire episode sitting lazily by the pool as if nothing peculiar were happening. The Great Dane caught her eye and whined.

"You've only been in this town for two days and you've already lost the old lady," the boy said bitterly, as he floated into the girls' path.

"We didn't lose her, she was taken by a monster as big as a mountain," Sabrina argued.

"Well, if you've come looking for help, you've come to the wrong place," the boy crowed. "Rescuing old ladies is a job for a hero! I'm a villain of the worst kind."

"Good! We don't want your help!" Sabrina said angrily, tossing the boy's sword aside.

"I thought Peter Pan was one of the good guys," Daphne added.

The boy's face turned so red Sabrina thought his head might explode. "Peter Pan? I'm not Peter Pan! I'm Puck!"

"Who's Puck?" Daphne asked.

"Who's Puck?" the boy cried. "I'm the most famous Everafter in this town. My exploits are known around the world!"

"I've never heard of you," Sabrina replied. She spun around and started walking through the yard to the street, with her sister and Elvis following. After only a couple of steps, the boy was hovering in front of them again.

"You've never heard of the Trickster King?" Puck asked, shocked.

The girls shook their heads.

"The Prince of Fairies? Robin Goodfellow? The Imp?"

"Do you work for Santa?" Daphne asked.

"I'm a fairy, not an elf!" Puck roared. "You really don't

know who I am! Doesn't anyone read the classics anymore? Dozens of writers have warned the world about me. I'm in the most famous of all of William Shakespeare's plays."

"I don't remember any Puck in *Romeo and Juliet*," Sabrina muttered, feeling a little amused at how the boy was reacting to his non-celebrity.

"Besides *Romeo and Juliet*!" Puck shouted. "I'm the star of *A Midsummer Night's Dream*!"

"Congratulations," Sabrina said flatly. "Never read it."

Puck floated down to the ground. His wings disappeared and he spun around on his heel, transforming into a big shaggy dog. Elvis growled at the sight of him, but Puck didn't attack. Instead, he shook himself all over, spraying the girls with water. When he was finished, he morphed back into a boy.

As she wiped the water off her face, Sabrina was tempted to give the weird boy another piece of her mind, but they had wasted enough time with this "Puck." She took Daphne's hand in hers once more, and together they marched down the deserted street.

"I'm afraid the old lady is a goner!" Puck taunted. "You'll get no help from me. Like I said, I'm a villain."

"Fine!" Sabrina shouted back.

"Fine!"

Daphne turned on the boy. "You sent those pixies to attack us last night, didn't you?"

"Just a little fun," Puck replied.

"That wasn't very nice." The little girl gave him her best angry look and then turned to join her sister.

"I'm a lot of things, but nice isn't one of them," the boy called after them.

"Maybe we should team up with him? He could fly over the forest and spot the giant," Daphne suggested to Sabrina.

"Daphne, you saw what a lunatic he is. I don't want him to ruin whatever slim chance we might have."

• • •

The path to the front door of Granny Relda's cottage seemed like a walk up a mountain, and by the time they arrived at the house Sabrina was nearly asleep standing up. She took out Granny's key ring and felt the weight of a hundred keys jingling in her hand, singing their mysteries.

By the time all the locks were open, it seemed as if hours had passed. Elvis was asleep and drooling on the sidewalk, swinging his thick legs back and forth as he dreamed.

As Sabrina unlocked the final lock, she turned to her sister and smiled. "That's all of them." She twisted the knob and leaned into the door. Unfortunately, the door didn't swing open. In fact, it didn't budge at all.

"What's wrong?" Daphne said, sitting up. She had been resting on the ground with her head on Elvis's warm belly.

"It's jammed," Sabrina said, pushing her shoulder against the big door to force it open.

Daphne got up and walked over. "Are you sure you unlocked them all?" she said. Sabrina fumed. If she knew anything, it was how to unlock a door. They'd escaped from a dozen foster homes in the last year and a half. Locks were not Sabrina's problem. She took the cold doorknob in her hand and turned it, proving that she had unlocked it. She pushed hard but still nothing happened.

"Well, it's not opening. Maybe the back door," she said, preparing to circle the house.

"You've forgotten the secret," a familiar voice commented. Puck floated to the ground, his huge wings disappearing just as he landed.

"What do you want?" Sabrina demanded.

"I did a flyby, all the way up into the mountains. I found some tracks, but no giant," Puck said. "I sent some pixies to keep searching without me."

Sabrina turned the doorknob angrily, hoping the door would suddenly open so she could laugh as she slammed it in Puck's face. But again, nothing happened.

"You have to tell the house you are home." Puck sighed.

"Of course!" Daphne knocked on the door three times. "We're home," she said, repeating the same words the girls had heard Granny Relda say each time they had entered the house, and turning the doorknob. The door finally swung open.

"How did you know that?" Daphne asked Puck.

"The old lady and I are close. She tells me everything."

Elvis immediately leaped to his feet and trotted into the house, nearly knocking over the girls on his way to the kitchen. The girls followed, and Puck pushed his way in as well, closing the door behind him.

"Now, I know I'm one of the bad guys," the boy said, tossing himself into the fluffy recliner in the living room. "But the old lady does provide me with a meal from time to time. Not that I feel any loyalty, but if she were to get eaten by a giant, my free lunches would disappear. So, we should probably get started."

"We? What do you mean *we*?" Sabrina cried.

"Of course, you two will have to keep this to yourselves," the boy continued, ignoring Sabrina. "I do have a reputation as the worst of the worst. If word got out that the Trickster was help-ing the heroes . . . well, it would be scandalous."

The girls stared at each other, dumbfounded.

"First things first. I want you two to prepare a hearty meal so that I will have plenty of energy to kill the giant," Puck instructed.

"You've got to be kidding," Sabrina groaned.

"The old lady always makes lunch when a mystery is afoot. I know it's not the most glamorous work, but I think you two are best suited for domestic tasks."

"What does *domestic tasks* mean?" Daphne asked.

"The way he means it is *women's work*," her sister replied.

Daphne snarled at the boy.

"Besides, as your leader I need to save my energy for the bat-tle," Puck insisted.

Sabrina's temper boiled over. "Leader! No one made you leader. No one even said they wanted your help!"

"You may not want it, but you need it," the boy shouted back. "The two of you can't even get into your own house. Do you think you'll strike fear into a giant?"

"Maybe if you two keep shouting, the giant will come to us," Daphne said.

Sabrina and Puck stared angrily at each other for a long moment.

"Who's hungry?" Daphne said. "I'm going to go do some domestic tasks for myself."

Sabrina was too hungry to fight any longer. Eating would clear her head. The three children raided the refrigerator and dug through the breadbox, grabbing anything and everything they thought they could eat. Puck seemed to share Daphne's big appetite; both of their plates were heaped with odd-colored food. The two also ate the same way—like hungry pigs, scarfing down anything that came close to their mouths. They were both working on seconds by the time Sabrina had made two Swiss cheese sandwiches and found what she hoped was just a weirdly colored apple.

"So, what's with the crown?" Daphne asked.

Puck's eyes grew wide. "I'm the Prince of Fairies. Emperor of Pixies, Brownies, Hobgoblins, Elves, and Gnomes. King of Tricksters and Prank-Players, spiritual leader to juvenile delinquents, layabouts, and bad apples."

The little girl stared at the boy with confusion in her face.

"I'm royalty!" Puck declared.

"So where's your kingdom?" Sabrina asked snidely.

"You're in it!" he snapped. "The forest and the trees are my kingdom. I sleep under the stars. The sky is my royal blanket."

"That explains the smell," Sabrina muttered.

The Trickster King ignored her comment and munched hungrily, tossing apple cores and whatever he couldn't eat onto the floor. A turkey bone soared from his hand and landed on a nearby windowsill.

"Puck, can I ask you a question?" Daphne said.

"You bet."

"If you knew Shakespeare, why do you look like you're only eleven years old?"

This was something Sabrina had been wondering about as well. Granny's explanation that magic kept the Everafters alive just wasn't making sense. Mayor Charming and Mr. Seven had to be hundreds of years old, yet they looked as if they hadn't aged at all.

"Ah, that's the upside of being an Everafter," Puck said. "You only get as old as you want to be. Some decided to age a little so that they could get jobs and junk like that."

"Then why didn't you?" Sabrina asked.

Puck shrugged. "Never crossed my mind. I plan on staying a boy until the sun burns out."

Sabrina thought that she'd like to see him running around in the dark as the earth froze over. She bit into her sandwich, only to discover that the Swiss cheese tasted more like hard applesauce.

"So, tell me what happened with the giant," said Puck.

While Sabrina ate, Daphne told the boy the whole sordid mess. She told him about the farmhouse that had been stepped on by the giant and how Mayor Charming had demanded that Granny Relda give up her detective work. How the farmer had spoken to a man named Mr. Englishman, and how a witch had erased the farmer's memory. She told about the gang of thugs that had attacked them outside of the hospital, and how, when they had followed the gang back to a cabin, they had spotted Charming again. Then she told him about the giant's attack, how he had killed the thugs, and how he had snatched up Granny and Mr. Canis.

Sabrina got up from her chair and went into the living room, where she stood in front of one of the many bookshelves.

"Books on giants . . . where would they be?" she said to herself. Puck and Daphne got up to join her, and together they scanned the bookcases.

"Look!" Daphne said.

Sabrina looked closely at the shelves Daphne was pointing to. They seemed to hold a collection of diaries. She took one down and read the title: *Fairy-Tale Accounts 1942–1965, by Edwin Alvin Grimm.*

"There's a book here for everyone in our family, I guess, including this one," said Daphne as she pulled one from the shelf and handed it to her sister. Sabrina almost dropped it when she eyed the title: *Fairy-Tale Accounts by Henry Grimm*. It was a book written by their father! She flipped through it, recognizing her dad's neat handwriting. She ran a finger along the short circles his words made, tracing his hand's movement from when he had put the words on paper. She turned more pages, feeling more of him in his words—not bothering to read, just taking comfort in knowing that he had once held the book.

"Let me see," Daphne said as she snatched the book from her sister's hands.

"You're wasting your time with these stupid books. I'm the smartest person I know and I've never read a book in my life. We should all be out looking," Puck said.

"If you want to go, there's nothing keeping you here," Sabrina said as she snatched her father's book back from Daphne. The two girls rushed to the dining room table and hovered over the slightly dusty journal. They flipped to the first page. A color photograph of Mayor Charming, dressed in royal gowns of purple-and-white silk, stared back at them. He wore a sapphire-and-diamond crown and a dazzling ruby ring on each finger. He smiled smugly, as if he thought very highly of himself.

Elvis sauntered into the room and licked Sabrina's hand. He spied Charming's picture and growled.

"Don't worry, Elvis! He can't get us now," Daphne said. Sabrina read aloud what her father had written.

July—Today we had another encounter with Charming. Mom and Dad discovered that he was attempting to buy a thousand acres of land on the eastern border of the town known as Old McDonald's farm. Where he got the money for such a big purchase came into question and Dad, of course, accused him of using his witches to conjure up phony cash. Charming huffed and demanded an apology. When Dad refused, the two of them got into a fistfight, which Charming got the worst of. (Dad has one heck of a left hook! KA-POW!) But the biggest surprise was Charming's freak-out. He swore he'd turn Ferryport Landing into his kingdom again, and he looked forward to the day when he could personally drive a bulldozer through our house.

"He's rebuilding his kingdom," Sabrina said as she flipped to the next page. There she found more interesting facts. "It's all in here. Listen to this."

December—Charming had given up the most when he

moved to America. He was forced to sell his castle, his horses, and everything he owned. One of the three ships Wilhelm had hired for the Atlantic crossing was used primarily to haul Charming's enormous fortune. The ship hit a sandbar off the coast of Maryland and sank, taking Charming's wealth to the bottom of the ocean. When he got to Ferryport Landing (changed from Fairyport Landing in 1910), he blew what was left on one bad investment after another: a failed diamond mine partnership with the seven dwarfs, a wholesale carpet company poorly managed by his business partner, Ali Baba, and a company that went bankrupt manufacturing something called a laser disc player. Being mayor doesn't pay much, and Dad believes that Charming runs a bunch of financial scams, both illegal and magical, just to keep the electricity on at the mayoral estate. That was until he came up with the greatest and most recent scam: the Ferryport Landing Fundraising Ball. Once a year, Charming invites the Everafter community to the mansion, and every year they throw money at him, trying to win his support for whatever political cause they have. The money obviously goes straight into the prince's pocket. I'd bet any-

thing that Charming is storing most of the money so that he can buy up the whole town and run it like his old kingdom.

"But what's that got to do with giants? And if he wanted to buy the farm, why did he send that Mr. Englishman to do the work?" Daphne asked.

"I believe that Mr. Englishman and Mayor Charming are the same person. Charming does have an English accent. He could have worn a disguise so Mr. Applebee wouldn't recognize him as the mayor," Sabrina said.

"I bet you're right!" her sister said.

"But where does the giant come in?" Sabrina wondered aloud.

"In the old days, giants and people used to work together all the time," Puck said, stealing the purple apple from Sabrina's plate and chomping on it.

"They did?"

"Oh yeah, giants are pretty dumb," the boy said. "From what I hear you can pretty much talk them into anything."

"He's right." Daphne was poring over a large book entitled *Anatomy of a Giant*. "I don't know what this word is," she said.

"How is it spelled?"

"A-L-L-I-A-N-C-E-S."

"It's *alliances*; it means to team up or join a group," Sabrina explained.

"It says that in olden days people used to form all-all . . ."

"Alliances."

". . . alliances with giants to destroy their enemies. People found that giants were very dumb and could be easily tricked."

"Charming's using the giant to scare people off their land. Anyone that won't sell gets squashed!" Sabrina cried.

"But you said he used Glinda to erase the farmer's mind, right?" Puck interrupted.

"Yes."

"Well, why would he do that? Why would he want the farmer to forget to be afraid?"

"And don't forget the lens cap," Daphne added. "If he were trying to scare them off, why would he want to videotape it? I don't think I'd want any proof of what I'd done if it were me."

Sabrina didn't have any more answers.

"Let me finish," her sister said, looking down at the book. "It also says that rarely do these all-all . . ."

"Alliances."

"Yeah, it says they usually backfire. In most cases, the human was eaten by the giant or dragged off to the giant kingdom to be a slave. There's a story here about a giant kidnapping a princess for an evil baron, and before the baron could collect a ransom from her family, the giant ate her," Daphne said quietly. "It says the townspeople used hound dogs to track down the giant because giants have a strong smell. When they caught him, he nearly killed the entire town before they could bring him down."

The girls spent a moment looking into each other's worried eyes. What if the giant had eaten Granny and Mr. Canis? What if he was eating them as they wasted time doing research?

"It says when giants got out of hand, the townspeople sent a hero to kill the giant for them," Daphne read. "His name was Jack and in his prime, he killed more than ten giants, stole treasure from the giant kingdom, and was world-famous."

Sabrina turned her attention back to her father's journal. She flipped through more of its pages until she found an envelope stuffed inside.

"What's this?" she wondered aloud.

Daphne got up from her chair and walked around the table to look.

"It says *To Sabrina, Daphne, and Puck. From Granny Relda*," Sabrina said.

"See! I told you I knew her!" Puck cried.

"Read it," Daphne begged.

Sabrina tore open the letter and began to read.

Lieblings,

If you're reading this, then one of my investigations has not turned out the way I had hoped. I don't want you to worry, as I am very experienced with all kinds of things and can take care of myself, and I know a little kung fu. If for some reason I am unable to be there and you need my help, you should take my keys and enter the room you have been forbidden to enter. All the answers you need will be staring you in the face.

Love, Granny Relda

P.S. Don't give Elvis any sausage. It makes him gassy.

"She wants us to go into the room?" Puck said in amazement. "I've been trying to get in there since the day she told me it was off-limits!"

"Cool! That's where she got that giant-detector she used at the farm," Daphne cried. "I bet the place is filled to the ceiling with stuff we can use to rescue them!"

"Staring us in the face? What does that mean?" Sabrina said, but before she knew it, her little sister was halfway up the stairs with the key ring in her hand.

"Wait up!" Sabrina shouted, taking the stairs two at a time. By the time she got to the top, Daphne was already trying keys.

"I bet she's got a shrink-ray in here. We'll shrink him down to the size of an ant and stomp on him," the younger girl said.

"Hurry," Sabrina said.

Puck flew up the stairs and grabbed the keys out of Daphne's hands.

"Royalty first, peasant."

"She gave these keys to us," Sabrina snapped, snatching the keys from him.

"A set of keys you have no idea how to use!" Puck shouted, taking them back.

"Puck, give me those keys!"

"No!"

"Listen Puck, don't make me do something you're going to regret."

"I've fought tougher guys than you, Grimm. Though most of them had better-smelling breath!"

"WHAT IS GOING ON OUT THERE?" a voice suddenly boomed from behind the door. It startled them all so much that they fell backward onto the floor.

"Did you hear that?" Daphne whispered.

"Everyone heard that," Sabrina and Puck replied.

"KNOCK OFF THAT RACKET RIGHT NOW!" the voice shouted angrily.

"Maybe it's the sheriff? Maybe he got into the house some-how?" Daphne whispered.

"Hamstead would have just come down and grabbed us," her sister said. "Besides, Elvis isn't freaking out."

"Then who is it?" Puck said.

"Granny locks that door for a reason. If there's someone in that room, Granny doesn't want them going anywhere. They might be dangerous," Sabrina warned.

"I'm not afraid!" the boy cried.

"I have an idea," Daphne said. She took Puck and Sabrina's hands and led them back down the stairs and into the kitchen.

• • •

Within minutes, the girls and Puck were standing at the bottom of the stairs again. Each was wearing a metal spaghetti strainer as a mighty battle helmet. Daphne wore an ancient washing board on her chest and had duct-taped huge metal spoons to each kneecap as protection from unfair kicks. She held a frying pan as her weapon. Sabrina had a pressure cooker lid taped to her behind. She held a wok pan for a shield and a rolling pin for a club. She swung it, preparing to whack whomever might be on the other side of the door. Puck had his trusty sword in one hand and a car-rot peeler in the other. He'd found a couple of cookie pans to tape to his chest and back, and his feet were encased in oven mitts.

The big dog stood behind them with an odd, confused expression.

"We should send Elvis up first," Sabrina said.

"Good idea," Daphne replied.

Sabrina turned to the Great Dane. "Elvis, there's someone upstairs. Go get him!"

Elvis sat down on his hind legs and used his back paw to scratch his neck. If he understood the order, he wasn't letting on. Discouraged, Sabrina turned back to her sister and Puck. "We'll go together and sneak up on him."

They nodded in agreement, and all three took the first step up the stairs. Their "armor" clanged and knocked around, causing a tremendous racket. By the time they got to the top of the steps, Sabrina realized that a sneak attack was probably no longer realistic, so she went with plan B.

"Whoever is up here better leave, 'cause we're armed to the teeth. I wouldn't want to be you when we find you!" Sabrina shouted. Her threat was met with silence.

"Maybe he's gone," Daphne said hopefully.

"I say we bust the door down and skin him alive," Puck said loudly.

"There's going to be no skinning of anyone," Sabrina said as she fumbled in her pocket and pulled out the key ring. She started the tedious work of finding the right key, and soon one went in the lock and clicked.

"Just stay together and, most of all, stay calm. If we don't panic, we can take this guy ourselves," Sabrina said.

"On three," Daphne whispered, giving her frying pan a practice swing.

"ONE, TWO, THREE!" Sabrina screamed, pushing the door open and rushing into the room. The trio swung their weapons frantically, slashing at whatever enemy dared to face their deadly kitchen utensils. After several minutes, and zero deadly hits, Sabrina stopped and looked around the room. In the moonlight from the single window, she could see it was empty, except for a wood-framed, full-length mirror that hung on a wall.

Puck, who was lying on the floor laughing hysterically, roared, "STAY CALM, YOU SAY?"

"Where did he go?" Daphne said, as she peered behind the door and found no one.

"Maybe we imagined it," Sabrina said, scowling at the boy's laughter. "C'mon, let's get back to work."

She turned to leave, but Daphne said, "Granny's note said that all the answers we need would stare us in the face." She pointed at the mirror.

"It's just a mirror," her sister argued.

"It can't hurt to take a look!" Puck said, and trotted over to it. Sabrina switched on the room light and reluctantly joined him, followed by Daphne, and together they looked at their reflection.

"I think I see something," Daphne said.

"What? What is it?" Sabrina said.

"A booger. It's in your nose." The little girl laughed. "Gotcha, again!"

Puck laughed so hard he snorted, but then saw Sabrina staring and stopped abruptly.

"WHO ARE YOU?" a loud voice suddenly bellowed from within the mirror. Sabrina looked into its reflection and felt the hairs on the back of her neck stand on end. A face was staring out at her but it was not her own. Floating without a body, the face was that of a man with a bald head and thick, angular features. He stared at the children with eyes like blue flames flickering a mixture of rage and disgust, as if the children were rodents found munching on the turkey during Christmas dinner. Terrified, the children ran back toward the door, but a blue ray shot from the mirror, hit the door, and slammed it shut, trapping them inside.

"WHO ARE YOU?" the head bellowed. "TELL ME NOW OR I WILL KILL YOU WHERE YOU STAND!"

7

'd like to see you try," Puck said defiantly.

A six-foot-high circle of fire snaked around the group, trapping them inside. The flames licked at the pots and pans the children had hoped would act as armor, and managed to scorch Sabrina's hand. She pulled it close to her and rubbed the painful burn.

"I WILL ROAST THE FLESH FROM YOUR BONES!" the face threatened. Dark gray clouds framed the bulbous head in a violent thunderstorm. Lightning crackled around the face, exploding in light and sound with every twitch of its eyebrows. "Who dares to invade my sanctuary?"

Sabrina pulled Daphne close to her, while Puck stepped between them and the closest flame, thrusting his little sword into the wall of fire. "We're not invaders! We live here!" he shouted over the roaring fire.

The face cocked an eyebrow and looked at them sternly.

"You're the grandchildren?"

"Yes! Sabrina and Daphne!" Sabrina shouted.

"And Puck!" Puck chimed in.

Suddenly, the fire puttered out, as if someone had turned off a stove.

"Oh, thank goodness. I thought carnival folk had broken into the house," the head cried. "You can hardly blame me, three kids break into my room and they're dressed like escaped inmates from the Ferryport Landing Asylum. You may not have heard, but the whole circus-clown-meets-crazy-street-vagrant-look is so over."

Sabrina looked down at her outfit: the torn, bright-blue pants, the orange sweatshirt with the monkey, the pressure-cooker lid strapped to her behind. Her face flushed with embarrassment as she took off her spaghetti-strainer helmet.

"What are you?" Sabrina asked, regaining her composure.

"I'm not a what, I'm a who!" the face in the mirror croaked, looking deeply insulted.

"Then who are you?" Sabrina said impatiently.

"Tsk, tsk, tsk, why I'm the seer of seers, the visionary of

visionaries, the man who puts the fun in your reflection," he replied with a dramatic flourish.

Sabrina looked at her sister for help. Daphne had read more fairy tales than Sabrina, but the little girl returned her sister's glance with a dumbfounded shrug. The face in the mirror frowned, sensing that the girls were far from star-struck and, in fact, had no idea who he was.

"I'm the magic mirror!" the face snapped.

"We could have guessed you were a magic mirror," Puck muttered.

"Not *a* magic mirror! *The* magic mirror! 'Mirror, mirror, on the wall'?"

"From 'Snow White'?" Daphne asked.

"Is there another?" The face growled. "You can call me *Mirror*. Your grandma told me you were coming from New York City, though she didn't tell me she was giving you a set of keys."

"She didn't. Granny threw hers to us before she was carried off by a giant," Daphne explained.

Mirror's eyes grew wide with astonishment.

"Well, there's a sentence you don't hear every day." He chuckled. "And I suppose you are in the midst of a rescue plan?"

"They are," Puck said defensively. "I'm a villain."

"So, let's hear this thrilling plan," said Mirror.

"We haven't got all the details worked out yet," Sabrina said, trying to make herself sound older and more mature.

"You don't have a plan!" Mirror exclaimed.

"We're still working on it," Sabrina muttered. "We thought there might be something up here that could help us."

"You're just like Henry." Mirror sighed. "Ready to jump headfirst into an adventure, hoping he'd come up with a plan along the way."

The girl was shocked. *Headfirst* didn't sound like her dad at all. *My dad read the labels on cans of food before everyone could eat,* she thought.

"You knew our father?" Daphne exclaimed.

"Knew him? I was Henry's babysitter most of the time. I saw him off to the prom. I was even invited to your parents' wedding. They propped me up on my own seat. I am a member of this family, after all."

"Sorry, we didn't mean to offend you," the little girl said. "So if you're *the* magic mirror, what do you do?"

"I can show you anything you want to see; all you have to do is ask," Mirror said proudly.

"What are you talking about?" Sabrina asked with growing impatience. All this chatter was keeping them from acting. Who knew what that monster was doing to Granny and Mr. Canis.

"You got a question. I got an answer," the face bragged. "All you got to do is ask."

"Are Granny Relda and Mr. Canis still alive?" Daphne asked.

"Sorry, kiddo, that's not how it works. You have to ask me the right way."

"What's the right way?" Sabrina demanded.

"Well, if you're going to be cranky, then just forget it!" Mirror said. He jutted out his lower lip.

Puck swung his carrot peeler menacingly at the face, then realized what he was doing, and flashed his little sword. "Listen, Mirror, you tell us what we want to know or you're going to find yourself cracked and broken all over the floor!"

"You wouldn't dare!"

"Just see if I wouldn't!"

Daphne tugged on Puck's arm. Acting as the diplomat for the group, she apologized to Mirror. "We're just very eager to find our granny and Mr. Canis, and we don't understand what you are saying."

The face's expression changed to a huge smile. "Apology accepted. Now, like I was going to say before I was so rudely interrupted," he said as he eyed Sabrina disapprovingly, "you have to ask your questions in a special way to activate the magic. You have to . . ."

"Rhyme them!" Daphne interrupted with a happy cry. "Bingo!"

The little girl turned to the other two. "We have to rhyme the question. Like, mirror, mirror, on the wall, who's the fairest of them all?"

A blue mist filled the mirror's surface and the face faded away, only to be replaced with the image of the most beautiful woman Sabrina had ever seen. She had black hair like Daphne's, and flawless, porcelain skin. She was standing in front of a classroom, teaching. Every boy in the class stared at her like a lovesick puppy, and there was a stack of apples on her desk.

"That would still be the lovely Snow White," Mirror said.

Just then, all the students got up from their seats and exited the room. When Snow White was finally alone, she tossed the apples into a garbage can and slid it under her desk.

"OK, how about this?" Sabrina said. "Mirror, mirror in a beehive, is Granny Relda still alive?"

The man in the mirror's face reappeared and he was frowning. "In a beehive?"

"All you said was it had to rhyme. You didn't say it had to make sense."

"Very well," said the face, and the blue mist returned. "Your grandmother is alive and well, for now."

"Where is she?" Daphne asked.

"Uh-uh. One question at a time, and that one didn't rhyme, anyway."

"Mirror, mirror we're just kids, can you show us where our grandma is?" Puck chimed in.

"Sorry, that doesn't technically rhyme," Mirror argued.

"It's close enough!" the children shouted.

Mirror frowned but misted over and, suddenly, Granny and Mr. Canis appeared in the reflection. They were climbing on top of their car, which was enclosed in what could only be described as a giant bag. Mr. Canis pulled the fabric down and the two of them looked over the edge. They were still in the giant's shirt pocket.

"They're alive." Daphne sighed with relief as the image zoomed out to show the giant. The ugly brute was asleep, lounging against a huge rock outcropping.

"He's up in the mountains," Puck said.

"You've probably tossed kids off of that very cliff," Sabrina commented.

"A few," Puck agreed, making Sabrina wonder if he was serious. "Look at the size of that beast. I'm going to need a bigger sword."

"We'll come with you," Daphne said.

"You aren't going anywhere," the boy replied. "The last thing

I need is a couple of girls bawling while I fight the giant. You two are staying here."

"What are we supposed to do while that's happening?" Sabrina asked.

"Women's work. You can clean up that mess in the dining room."

"Women's work!" the girls cried.

"Oh, you've said it now," Mirror warned Puck.

"If anyone's going up there, it's me!" Sabrina declared. "I can't expect some smelly kid who lives in the woods to save my grandmother. You couldn't even push me into a pool. You stay here and keep an eye on Daphne!" she commanded.

"'Keep an eye on Daphne?'" Daphne repeated indignantly. "I'm not staying here! She's my granny, too!"

"What you need is someone who has had experience with giants," Mirror interrupted.

"What we need is someone who can kill a giant," Sabrina said.

"Like the Big Bad Wolf," Daphne suggested.

"No, tougher than that."

"I'll do it!" Puck said angrily. It was obvious that the boy was offended at their lack of respect for his fighting skills.

"Mirror, mirror, what can we do, to rescue Granny from you know who?" Sabrina asked.

The mirror misted over once again, and this time when it cleared the children saw a man sitting in a jail cell. He had a boyish face with spiky blond hair and big eyes. He was lying lazily on a thin, ratty cot. He got up, walked over to a small window, looked out, pulled on the bars in a hopeless effort to free himself, and when he found them unbendable, scowled and returned to his dingy bed.

"You need the help of Jack the Giant Killer," Mirror said, as his face returned to the reflection.

"Jack the Giant Killer?" Sabrina asked.

"'Jack and the Beanstalk,'" Daphne explained. "He's the same guy."

"That guy sitting in jail has killed giants? I'm not impressed," Puck said, continuing his sulk.

"Granny said he was down on his luck," Sabrina said. "But I didn't think she meant *that* down. I guess it'll be easy to find him now."

"We passed the jailhouse on the way to the hospital," her sister pointed out.

"We do not need Jack," Puck fumed.

Suddenly, Elvis barked an angry warning from downstairs. It was followed by several loud knocks on the front door.

"Who's that?" Sabrina whispered.

"Mirror, mirror, one question more, who's that knocking on our door?" Daphne asked.

"Now you're getting the hang of it!" Mirror said as his face misted over. Outside of the house, two police cars were parked in the driveway. "It seems as if the local authorities have arrived."

"Hamstead's here," Sabrina said as the image revealed the fat sheriff hoisting up a new pair of pants in between angry knocks on the front door. An equally plump deputy with a thick handlebar moustache gestured for Hamstead to walk around the house, and together they did, revealing pink curly tails sticking out of the backs of their beige slacks.

"He brought friends," Daphne said as the image blurred, then reappeared from another angle. Another equally rotund deputy with a shock of bright, white hair tucked under his hat walked along the side of the house, trying to find an open window. When he got to the dining room window, he placed his face against it to peer in, only to fall over backward when Elvis lunged at him from the other side. The terrified deputy transformed into a pig, but changed back once he calmed down.

"Ferryport's finest, Sheriff Hamstead and his dim-witted deputies, Swineheart and Boarman," said Mirror.

"I can't believe the Three Little Pigs are working for the bad guy." Daphne sighed.

"I can't believe anyone still calls them the three *little* pigs." Mirror tittered. "That trio has been tipping the scales for as long as I can remember."

"Look at them, they're no match for us. Why, I could take the three of them by myself," Puck said so excitedly that his wings appeared and he flew off the floor. Sabrina pulled him back down by his sweatshirt sleeve.

"Ladies, this is the police. Open the door," the sheriff demanded through a megaphone in a tinny, amplified voice. "We can stay out here all night if we have to."

"What do we do?" Daphne asked.

"Nothing. They can't get in here," Puck replied.

"But we can't get out. We're trapped," Sabrina said, worried.

"What is this nonsense I'm hearing from you?" Mirror said. "You two are Grimms. Performing the impossible is what you do. Do you think your family could have survived this long with ogres and monsters running around if they couldn't find a way out of their own house?"

"OK, you're so smart, *you* tell us what to do," Sabrina snapped. "We came up here because we're looking for some help. Now there are cops outside who want to arrest us and, worse, who are keeping us trapped in here so we can't get out and save our grandmother and her best friend, who have been kidnapped by a giant!"

"You're asking for my help?"

"Yes! Do we have to rhyme it, too?"

"Not at all. Ask, my little wardrobe-challenged friends, and you shall receive," the face said. "I need your keys."

"What? Why?" Sabrina asked.

"Do you want some help or not? Give me the keys." The reflection warped, and a portion of the mirror's surface grew outward as if someone were blowing a bubble from the other side. It pushed out farther and farther, causing the reflection to shimmer and ripple until a hand was thrust through. Even Puck seemed unsettled by what he was seeing.

"C'mon, girl, I don't have all night," Mirror complained.

Sabrina put the keys into the hand and it disappeared into the bubble.

"I'll be right back," the face said as it vanished and the surface of the mirror flattened, returning to normal. After several moments, the face reappeared.

"I've got just the thing for you," Mirror said with a smile. Again, the surface of the glass rippled, and this time a dusty, rolled-up carpet came through. Once it had completely broken the surface, the carpet fell to the ground, where it unrolled before them.

Dazzling burgundy and gold threads formed an intricate pattern of symbols: moons, stars, flowers, sickles, and triangles, which seemed to shimmer as if they were woven from precious metal. Golden roped tassels hung from the carpet's edges. Sabrina thought it was the most beautiful rug she had ever seen.

"What's this?" Daphne said, stepping on the carpet. Suddenly it lifted off the floor and hovered in the air. The movement was so quick that Daphne fell onto her backside. "It flies!"

"Just a little thing your grandpa picked up during a trip to the Middle East. Maybe you've heard of Aladdin?" Mirror said proudly. "This is his flying carpet. Thought it might be the best thing for your little rescue mission. Just tell it the location of where you want to go and it'll get you there. Even if you don't know how to get there yourself."

"How do I make it go down?" Daphne asked, giggling, but no sooner had the question left her lips than the carpet fell to the ground, causing Daphne's "armor" to clang on the floor.

"When you're finished with it, I expect you to return it," said Mirror sternly as Granny's keys came back through the surface and fell to the ground. Sabrina picked them up.

"But how are we going to get out of the house?" Sabrina asked.

"Listen, cowgirl, I can't do it all for you. From what I hear, you're quite the expert at being sneaky. I suggest you cause a diversion," Mirror said.

"With what?"

"I don't know. What could possibly distract three pigs enough so that you could get away?"

Sabrina thought for a moment and then grinned. "I know exactly what to do."

• • •

The girls carried the carpet down the stairs and into the kitchen, where they laid it on the floor. They removed their "armor," and Sabrina opened the refrigerator. Granny's odd and abundant cooking filled the shelves. It would take an army to eat it all. The girls pulled out pies, cakes, oddly colored fruits, and several things Sabrina couldn't identify, and tossed them onto the carpet. Elvis sat by, drooling with hunger, obviously wondering what they were doing.

"Is this enough?" Daphne asked.

"I hope so," Sabrina answered. "Carpet, up!"

The carpet rose to her waist and hovered next to her. "Come!" she commanded, and the carpet followed them as they walked to the front door.

Daphne peeked out the window. "They're sitting on the hoods of their squad cars," she said. "Puck, are you ready?"

The boy entered the foyer. He had finished taking off the last of his own kitchen gear and now pulled a small flute from his sweatshirt pocket.

"You don't have to ask the Trickster King if he is ready," he said arrogantly.

"I'm ready," Daphne said to Sabrina. "But are you sure about this? The police are after us. Do you think going to the jailhouse is the smartest thing?"

"I don't see any other way," Sabrina said as she opened up the front door. Hamstead scrambled off the car hood.

"Finally, you two have come to your senses," he said as he and his deputies approached the house.

Sabrina looked down at the carpet full of food hovering next to them. "Carpet, go to the policemen," she said. The carpet rose into the air and floated gently toward Hamstead and his men, and as it got closer it began to have the effect Sabrina had hoped for.

"Food!" one of the deputies squealed as the carpet stopped at their feet. The smell of the cakes and pies sent a change through the two men, and soon both were in pig form, rooting wildly through the banquet the girls had built on the rug.

"Gentlemen, we have work to do here!" Hamstead shouted while eyeing a pan of baked beans the others had overlooked. Unable to resist, he quickly shape-shifted to his pig form and slopped around in the mess.

Puck hovered several feet in the air near the girls, clearly displeased with Sabrina's success.

Daphne looked up at him and smiled. "We couldn't do this without you," she said, earning a grumpy shrug. "As soon as Jack tells us how to stop that giant, we're going to need you to lead us again."

The boy puffed up with pride, and a huge smile sprang to his face. He winked at Daphne, and then zipped across the front yard until he was hovering directly over the squad cars. The gorging piggies didn't even notice him.

Sabrina, Daphne, and Elvis stepped out of the house, closing the door behind them. With nimble fingers, Sabrina went to work locking all the bolts on the door, while Daphne kept an eye on Hamstead and his men.

"They're disgusting," Daphne said, mimicking the pigs' grunting and oinking.

"OK, that's the last one," Sabrina said, inserting the final key. She turned it and heard the lock roll into place.

"Ready?" she asked, pulling up the zipper on her sister's jacket.

"Ready!"

Sabrina turned to the pigs. "Carpet, here!" she shouted.

Abruptly, the carpet pulled itself out from under the three pigs, sending them topsy-turvy and flopping across the yard. The food flew into the air and rained down on them with a great splat as the carpet itself glided across the yard and stopped at Sabrina's feet.

"Get them!" Hamstead shouted as he struggled onto his hoofs and then back into his human form. The deputies followed suit and in no time they were all running toward the girls.

"Excuse me, piggies," Puck called from above. He blew a low note on his flute and within seconds a wave of pixies flew out of the woods. He played another note and the little lights encircled the two parked squad cars.

"You know what to do," Puck called to the pixies and they went into action, effortlessly lifting each car. They carried them high over the house and into several large trees, where they squeezed them between the thick branches. The police officers snorted their protests, but the boy just laughed.

The plan was working, and it was time for the girls to go. They stepped onto the carpet.

"Hold on tight. We haven't actually ridden on this thing," Sabrina said. She and Daphne knelt down and each grabbed a side of the carpet. Elvis hopped on, too, and Daphne wrapped her free arm around his neck.

"Don't worry Elvis. I've got you," the little girl said.

The police had stopped watching the pixies steal their cars and were now closing in on the sisters. They were almost on top of them when Sabrina shouted, "UP!" and the carpet rocketed into the sky. The girls held on for their dear lives as the house, the yard, and even their street became smaller and smaller. Sabrina's stomach lurched as they found themselves shooting through a cloud.

"Carpet, down!" she said as the oxygen began to seep from her lungs. Just as quickly as the carpet rose, it fell. Daphne's pigtails lifted from the side of her head and floated next to her ears as the girls screeched back toward Earth, falling like a rock.

"CARPET, STOP!" Sabrina cried, inches before the carpet smashed onto the ground. She gasped with relief. Unfortunately, they had stopped right behind the three police officers, who were still searching the sky for the girls.

"Wait, we've forgotten something!" Daphne cried. "Carpet, take us to the front door."

"No!" Sabrina shouted, but it was too late. The magic carpet zipped off again, this time plowing into the group of portly police and knocking them down like bowling pins.

"What are you doing?" she demanded as the carpet screeched to a halt at the door of Granny's house.

"There's one more lock," Daphne said. She knocked on the door three times. "We'll be back!"

But the detour had given Hamstead and his men the time they needed to recover and they now had the carpet surrounded. Hamstead grabbed one of the tassels and smiled.

"OK, fun time is over, ladies," he said.

"Let go of the carpet," Sabrina demanded. Elvis echoed her protest with a low growl.

"Not a chance, girls! Now, let's head down to the station and . . ."

"I said, let go of the carpet."

"What are you going to do to make me?" Hamstead scoffed.

Sabrina and Daphne exchanged glances. Daphne tightened her grip on the carpet and gave an extra squeeze to Elvis at the same time.

"Carpet, up!"

The carpet shot into the sky, carrying the girls, Elvis, and a stubborn Hamstead with it. Hanging on with one hand, the sheriff desperately tried to climb on board as they soared high above the house.

"Take us down, right now!" he squealed.

Sabrina peeked over the side and smirked.

"I'm sorry, Sheriff, but you don't have a ticket for this flight. I'm afraid you're going to have to get off at the next stop. Carpet, we have an unwanted passenger. Get rid of him!"

The carpet bolted forward as if thrilled with the request. It zipped up and down and did wide loopty-loops that made Sabrina want to barf. She looked over at Daphne and Elvis, who both sat calmly on the carpet.

"If you just let go, it's a real easy ride," Daphne shouted over the whipping wind, but Sabrina wasn't convinced, and held on tightly. A small beetle flew into her mouth and she spit it out, gagging.

"A bug flew in my mouth!" Sabrina croaked. Daphne patted her hand sympathetically.

Unfortunately, Hamstead was still very much a passenger.

"Let go!" Sabrina shouted again, but the sheriff shook his head defiantly. Displaying its own stubbornness, the carpet darted over the house and began to skim the top of the forest. Hamstead smacked into limbs and skittered across the treetops.

"I'm not going anywhere," he shouted as the carpet found an opening in the forest and dove into it like a kamikaze pilot. Sabrina was sure the carpet was going to sacrifice them all to get rid of its unwanted rider, but just as it seemed they would all be splattered across the forest floor, the carpet leveled out and dragged Hamstead directly over some thorny bushes. Motivated by the pain, the sheriff struggled once more to climb on board. Elvis barked at him as Daphne tried to pry his fingers from the carpet's tasseled corner.

"Carpet, do something!" she cried.

The carpet soared between several trees and zipped along a rocky stream. It lowered itself to mere inches above the water,

dragging Hamstead along the muddy banks, and finally shaking him loose. He tumbled into the mud and sank up to his nose.

The carpet darted back and hovered above him. The sheriff crawled out of the muck, covered in swamp goo. A small frog leaped from his shirt pocket as he wiped filth from his eyes.

As the girls darted away on the carpet, Sabrina could hear Boarman and Swineheart rushing to their boss's aid.

"Boss, what are you fooling around in the mud for?" Boarman asked.

"Shut up!"

The girls soared out of the forest and high into the sky. There, Puck met them and flew alongside, laughing at the sheriff's misfortune.

"You keep them busy!" Sabrina shouted and the boy's mood darkened.

Daphne pinched her sister. "You have to talk to him like he's the leader. He needs to feel that he's important," Daphne whispered.

Sabrina was stunned by her sister's perceptiveness. "Sorry, Puck, I know you can handle them and we'll be back soon with all the information you will need," Sabrina said awkwardly. "We know you could kill the giant yourself right now, but a little insider information never hurts."

Again, Puck puffed up with pride. "Of course, probably a waste of time, but who knows? By the way, there's one more cop you have to deal with when you get there."

"Who?" Daphne asked.

"A nervous little man named Ichabod Crane."

"Not the guy from Sleepy Hollow?" Sabrina said.

"That's him. Since he nearly lost his head, he gave up teaching and became a cop. I guess his idea is that he's safer if he's around the police. He shouldn't be too much of a problem," Puck said, turning in midair and soaring away.

"How did you know that we could get him to do whatever we want if we pretended he's in charge?" Sabrina asked Daphne.

"It's what I do with you," the little girl replied. "You two are exactly the same."

"Carpet, take us to Jack," Sabrina said after she had stuck her tongue out at her sister.

The carpet darted on and glided above the little town. For the first time, Sabrina could see Ferryport Landing for what it really was—quaint. To the east of the town, the moon shone on the curve of the Hudson River, and old gas lamps lined the paths of a park along the water. More lights twinkled in the center of the town, where dozens of brownstone buildings clustered around Main Street. Sabrina could see people having a late supper in the railway-car diner and a last movie playing at the drive-in theater. Far off to the west of town, she could just make out the humped shapes of the tree-blanketed mountains.

As they got closer to Main Street, the carpet began to descend, dropping nearly a dozen feet at once and causing Sabrina's belly to flip. She looked at her sister and saw that she had wrapped her arms around Elvis and was squeezing the air out of the poor dog. They plummeted through the clouds, the girls screaming as the wind screeched past them, but just as they were feet from crashing onto the pavement, Sabrina managed to shout "Carpet, STOP!" and the carpet screeched to a halt. It took them several moments to realize that they hadn't died and that they were still screaming.

When they had calmed down, Sabrina looked around and saw that they were floating next to the window of a brick building. It had bars on it. Suddenly, a boyish-looking head with spiky blond hair appeared. It was Jack! He had beautiful blue eyes and a round face with a button nose, but he looked tired and in desperate need of a shave. He also had a painful-looking fat lip that had specks of dried blood around it.

"What is going on out there? Can't a man get some rest when he's in prison?" he shouted in a thick English accent. When he saw the girls, he lifted himself higher in order to see what they were standing on. Then he smiled.

"Well, young ladies. Who might you be?"

"Are you Jack?" Sabrina asked.

"That's the name I was given," he replied with a chuckle.

"*The* Jack?" Daphne asked. "As in 'Jack and the Beanstalk'?"

"Indeed I am, duck. But as you can see, I'm a little indisposed to be signing autographs." He laughed.

"We need your help!" Daphne cried.

"Well, I don't know if you happened to have noticed, but this isn't a country club I'm relaxing in. This is the county jail. Unless you need some help making license plates, I think you've got the wrong bloke."

"We need your help with a giant," Sabrina said.

Jack's eyes grew wide and a smile briefly lit up his features. Then he grew terribly serious and pulled his face closer to the bars.

"A giant, you said?"

"He's taken our grandmother," Sabrina replied.

"And we want her back!" Daphne added.

"Well, I don't blame you," the young man said. "But exactly how does a human go about getting themselves in trouble with a giant?"

"We're Sabrina and Daphne Grimm. Our grandmother is . . ."

"Relda Grimm," Jack interrupted with a smirk. "I should have guessed. Went and got herself in trouble with a big boy, eh?"

"Yes, she and Mr. Canis both," Daphne said.

"Canis, eh? Can't say I feel sorry about that," Jack growled. "So what do you want from me?"

"We were told you were an expert on giants," Sabrina answered. "We need you to tell us everything you can about how to stop this one and save our family."

"It's true, I am an expert on the big boys. Killed nearly fifty of them in my day," Jack boasted.

"The books said it was less than twenty," Daphne said.

"Don't believe everything you read, duck," said Jack. "I've sent more than my fair share of big boys to the grave. Why, there was a time when people used to call me *Jack the Giant Killer*. I was famous, oh yes. My name was once synonymous with bravery and daring. That was until the spell that trapped me in this barmy town."

"What does *barmy* mean?" Daphne whispered to her sister.

Sabrina shrugged. She was having trouble keeping up with Jack's accent.

"Now I'm taking any work I can. Do you know what the mighty Jack does for a living?"

Sabrina began to get nervous as the young man's face filled with rage. She knew the answer to his question but thought it best to lie. "No, I don't."

"I sell shoes and suits at Harold's House of Big and Tall," Jack exploded. "A lowly sales boy! I sat with kings. I drank the finest wines in the world. I filled my belly with exotic meats and socialized with the world's most interesting people and now, because of that cursed spell that keeps us here, I spend my days measuring inseams and helping people pick out insoles!"

"We're sorry," Daphne said.

"At least that's what I used to do. Today I quit!" Jack bragged. "I have a feeling Jack the Giant Killer's luck is going to change."

"So how did you end up in jail?" Sabrina asked.

"That miserable cur, Charming," Jack raged. "Runs this town like it's his own personal kingdom and wants to keep the rest of us as peasants."

"Did he give you the fat lip?" asked Sabrina.

"No . . . I had a disagreement with some business associates," Jack said, wiping his wound with a bloody handkerchief. "No worries. You can't keep a bloke like me down, can you? No-siree-bob! You can count on that!"

"Jack, I hate to interrupt, but we've really got to hurry. Is there anything you can tell us that will help?" Sabrina said.

"Oh, I'm going to be a big help to you ladies," he said with a confident grin. "Just as soon as the two of you break me out of jail."

 abrina gasped.

"You want us to help you break out of prison?"

Jack nodded his head. "Quite right."

"How are we supposed to do that?" Sabrina asked.

"Easy, you go in through the front door and distract the guard. Then the little one here will hit him in the gob with a club or something and snatch his keys."

"I'm seven years old. I can't hit someone with a club, and not in the gob—whatever that is!" Daphne cried.

"Sure you can. Deputy Crane isn't going to put up a fight. He's daft in the head and jumpy as a flea. But if he does happen to put up a fight, all you have to do is hit him in the shins. He'll fall over like a sack of potatoes," Jack replied.

"She's not hitting anyone with a club," Sabrina said.

"Well, if saving your granny and her pal isn't that important to you, I can just stay in the nick."

Sabrina looked into Jack's hopeful face. How could this odd little man actually be the key to Granny and Mr. Canis's survival? It just didn't seem possible, but on the other hand, the note Granny had left told them that the mirror would have all the answers they needed. After two days of disbelieving everything the old woman had told her, Sabrina didn't feel like being proven wrong again, especially when so much was riding on the outcome.

"So girls, what's it going to be? If I could do it myself, I would have already, but the bobby took my lock-picking kit when he put the cuffs on me. Smart on his part, too. There isn't a door Jack can't open."

"You say there's only one deputy?"

"Yes," Jack insisted.

"And he happens to be Ichabod Crane—the guy from 'The Legend of Sleepy Hollow'?"

"Not so much a legend as a true story, but yes."

"We'll get you out of here, but we're going to do it my way," Sabrina declared. "No one is going to get hurt. Deal?"

Jack frowned but thrust his hand out the window. He shook Sabrina's and smiled. "So boss, what's the plan?"

"First, I'm going to need your shirt."

• • •

When Sabrina opened the front door to the police station, her heart was pounding faster than it had ever pounded. They were taking a huge chance, especially with Sheriff Hamstead and his deputies searching for them. By now Crane had to know the girls were on the loose. Two kids dressed in bright-orange monkey sweatshirts, flying around on a magic carpet with a two-hundred-pound Great Dane weren't going to be too hard to spot. On the upside, what they were about to do was the sneakiest thing the girls had ever tried. It was nice to be challenged every once in awhile.

When the door swung open, Sabrina half expected to find Hamstead, Boarman, and Swineheart waiting for them. But luckily, the station was empty except for a tall, painfully thin man with a gigantic hooked nose, thin lips, and an Adam's apple that bobbed up and down. Ichabod Crane looked just like the story had described him, and he was fast asleep, sitting in a chair with his feet propped up on his desk.

Sabrina found the light switch and flipped it off, drowning the room in murkiness. She gestured behind her and the carpet drifted in, hovering two feet off the ground and carrying its own Headless Horseman: Daphne, sitting on Elvis's back and wearing Jack's shirt so that her head was hidden inside.

"He's going to figure this out," Daphne whispered.

"It's our only shot," Sabrina replied. She crouched down behind an empty desk and cupped her hands around her mouth. She used her feet to kick the door shut and it slammed so loudly the poor man fell backward over his chair. Once he was on his hands and knees, he rubbed his eyes and looked around in the dark.

"Hey, who turned out the lights?" he called in a whiny, high-pitched voice.

"Crane!" Sabrina moaned in the deepest voice she could produce. The carpet slowly drifted across the room, carrying its headless passenger.

"You!" the deputy cried in horror. "You're supposed to be gone!"

"I have returned," Sabrina croaked. The dark room was creating a very believable nightmare. Crane scurried around the room, hiding behind desks and chairs the best he could.

"Crane, you cannot hide from me. I am the Headless Horseman. I see all!"

The deputy screamed and continued to crawl, but the carpet hunted him slowly around the room.

"I'm a law enforcement officer now!" Crane shouted, trying to muster all his courage. "A defender of the peace. I can arrest you for . . . for . . . riding a horse without a head. That's a serious crime in this town," he cried.

"Your laws mean nothing to me. I've come for something, Crane, and I will have it!" Sabrina bellowed.

"What do you want?" the deputy cried.

"Your head!" Sabrina groaned.

Crane burst into tears. "No! Please, not my head!" he begged.

"Very well, if not your head, I'll take something else."

"Anything, anything. Whatever you want!"

"I want the keys to the jail."

Crane was silent for several moments.

"Why do you want the keys?"

"Would you prefer I take your head instead?" Sabrina moaned just as an unlucky bounce of the carpet knocked Daphne off Elvis's back. She fell to the ground, knocking a trash can into a radiator. The sound couldn't have been more appropriate, but Daphne was down for the count. Unable to see, she flailed in her costume, causing more commotion and sending a computer crashing to the floor.

Crane, who seemed to think this was part of the Headless Horseman's attack, shouted, "Here, the keys!" and tossed them at Daphne's feet.

"Now go, or I will change my mind!" Sabrina said. Crane

leaped to his feet and ran, not noticing Sabrina as he rushed out the station door. Once she was sure he was gone, Sabrina stood up and turned on the lights. Daphne was still rolling around, unable to see anything.

"Get me out of this," the little girl cried. Sabrina unhooked the top buttons and Daphne's head popped out. Elvis, who had stepped off the carpet, was ready with a lick to her face.

"You were very convincing." Sabrina laughed as she helped her sister to her feet.

Daphne reached down and scooped up the keys. "Let's get him out of here."

Sabrina rolled up the carpet, flung it over her shoulder, and the two girls raced to find Jack's cell.

Down a long hallway at the back of the building were two jail cells. The one on the left was empty, but the one on the right held Jack. He stood with his arms reaching through the bars as the girls entered the room.

"Give me the keys," he pleaded, but before they could, Elvis lunged angrily at the cell. Growling and barking wildly, the big dog sniffed and snarled at Jack.

"Elvis, it's OK, he's a friend," Daphne said, which seemed to calm the dog down, but still his nose was sniffing and at full alert.

Sabrina handed Jack the keys and he sorted through them.

"Corking! I told you it would work," he bragged.

He found the right key, stuck it in the lock, and turned it from inside. The door clicked and he pushed it open.

"Crane ran like he'd seen the devil himself," Sabrina said proudly.

"I've seen the devil, and you're not him," a voice said from down the hallway.

Sabrina turned and found Deputy Crane standing in the doorway, blocking their exit. He was so angry he was shaking.

"Listen, Crane, just let us pass and no one will get hurt," Jack said.

"Get back in your cell, Jack," the deputy ordered, pulling his billy club from its strap and swinging it threateningly.

"Sorry, Ichy. I wish I could help you but I've just been hired for a rescue mission. Now, are you going to let us pass or are we going to have to get rough?" Jack threatened.

Daphne grabbed his undershirt and yanked on it. "You promised, no one gets hurt."

Jack scowled. "I wouldn't hurt him . . . badly," he said.

"Do your worst!" Crane stammered as he backed up a step.

"Crane, I mean it. I'm not staying in this jail."

"Bring it on, you washed up has-been."

Jack laughed. "That's what I am? A washed up has-been? I'd

watch what you say, Ichy. Things can change in the blink of an eye."

"Not in Ferryport Landing, Jack."

The two stared at each other for a long time. Sabrina could almost feel the heat and rage in their eyes.

"Carpet, let's wrap this up!" Jack commanded and the carpet lifted off Sabrina's shoulder. It darted down the hallway and, like an anaconda, wrapped Crane inside it. He fumbled and fought but couldn't break free.

Jack walked over to the rug and patted it lightly.

"Nothing personal, Ichy, but destiny awaits," he said. He grabbed an end of the carpet and pulled it roughly, causing Crane to spin away like a top. After several rotations, the skinny man collapsed to the floor, overcome by dizziness. Jack set the carpet on the floor and stepped onto it.

"All right, ladies," he said as he extended his hand to help the girls onto the rug. Elvis rushed to join them and stood like a guard between the girls and Jack.

"Carpet, up," Sabrina said, and it rose a few feet and then sank slowly back down like a balloon with a hole in it.

"Why aren't we going up?" Sabrina cried.

"We must be too heavy!" Jack groaned. "Can we lose the hound?"

Elvis answered him with a threatening snarl.

"Very well. Carpet, take us to the Grimm house!"

Though it was weighed down, the carpet didn't lack any of its speed. It zipped along, three feet off the floor, down the hallway, through the main room, and out the front door of the police station. It sailed across the parking lot and made a left into the street, causing a pickup truck to screech to a stop. As they passed, the girls waved a friendly "sorry" gesture to the bewildered driver.

"That was almost too easy," Jack said. But no sooner had he puffed out his chest than the sound of a police siren wailed in their ears. A moment later, a police car turned the corner and raced in the group's direction. Ichabod Crane was behind the wheel.

"Tenacious, isn't he?" Jack said.

"Tenacious?" Daphne asked.

"It means persistent," Sabrina said.

"And what does *persistent* mean?" Daphne asked.

"It means he's not going to give up."

"And I wouldn't have it any other way," Jack assured them. "Carpet, faster!"

Close behind, Crane turned on his squad car's flashing lights.

"Is this the best idea?" Sabrina shouted, holding on to an end of the carpet as they sailed between cars and ran through a red light. "We're attracting a lot of attention!"

"It's about time this little burg saw some action!" Jack cried out happily. "Ferryport Landing, you haven't seen anything yet!"

Sabrina heard a horrible crunching sound behind them and turned back to see what could have made such a loud noise. What she saw stole the breath from her lungs. The road behind them began to rise, like a massive wave rolling in from the ocean. It was followed by another horrible crunching sound.

"What's happening?" she cried as she watched parked cars get tossed aside like toys.

"We're in luck, ladies," Jack said. "We've already found our giant."

Suddenly, a giant foot planted itself in the middle of Main Street. The impact caused windows in nearby businesses to shatter. The ground exploded and a gas main underneath the street burst, shooting flames high into the air.

"What do we do?" Daphne said.

"We have two choices. Stand and fight and die a horrible, messy death, or run," Jack said.

"Carpet, get us out of here!" Sabrina shouted, and the little rug jumped in speed.

Unfortunately, the giant was not discouraged by how fast the group was making its getaway. A single stride put the monster right behind them, even when the rug increased its speed again. And with every step the big monster took, the pavement crumbled beneath him. Electrical wires snapped, spraying sparks everywhere. The few drivers on the road at that early hour lost control of their cars and crashed into buildings. Jack turned to see the chaos and a broad grin came to his face.

"Finally, this is getting interesting." He laughed.

The carpet took a sharp left turn and Sabrina felt lucky that she hadn't tumbled off, when she noticed that Daphne was no longer sitting next to her. In fact, Daphne was hanging from the back of the carpet, holding on desperately with both hands.

"Jack!" Sabrina cried. The spiky-haired "legend" reached down and grabbed the little girl by the back of her sweatshirt and pulled her onto the carpet.

"Blimey! This is better than a roller coaster." Jack laughed as he sat the girl safely on the carpet.

Daphne hugged her sister. It was the first time Sabrina had ever felt her sister shake from fear. She didn't like it.

"We're going to get ourselves killed," she shouted as the carpet narrowly missed being crushed by a delivery truck filled with chickens.

"Nonsense, we can't die like this. We're immortal," Jack replied.

"You're immortal, we're not. We have to get off this road," Sabrina demanded.

"I see. Must be quite a pain to be human, but the carpet picks the route." Just then an eighteen-wheeler pulled directly into their path and stopped.

"CARPET, UP!" everyone shouted. The carpet slowly rose, sputtering as if it were the little train that couldn't.

"We're not going to make it!" Sabrina shouted.

"Lie down flat," Jack commanded.

"You can't mean what I think you mean!"

Jack nodded, and the two girls reluctantly lay on their backs.

"Elvis, play dead," Daphne said, and the dog lay on his side. The little girl turned a worried face to her sister. "He's not going to do what I think he is, is he?"

"CARPET, DOWN!" Jack shouted, and the carpet fell from the sky until it was literally skidding across the pavement. Its momentum carried the group underneath the truck to the other side and down the street. When they sat up again, the young man was already laughing—until he looked up and saw the street cleaner barreling toward them.

"CARPET, UP!" they all shouted and the little rug struggled higher, narrowly missing the boiling-hot water and sharp bristles the machine used to scour the street. The carpet continued to rise until it had cleared the vehicle. Sabrina sat up and turned around. Ichabod Crane was out of his car, angrily ordering the owners of the eighteen-wheeler and the street cleaner to move. Unfortunately, the traffic problems did little to stop the giant. It's monstrous foot soared high above the commotion and landed only yards from the carpet.

"THAT THING IS GOING TO KILL SOMEONE," Sabrina shouted. "Carpet, we have to get away from the main road!"

The carpet made an abrupt turn toward Ferryport Landing's farm community. The giant followed closely behind and the little rug dodged each deadly footfall. Several times the ugly brute reached out to squash the group in his hands, but each time the carpet zipped out of his reach. He grunted and roared at them, but eventually became exhausted by the chase and gave up, shaking his fist into the air and roaring with frustration.

"Don't cry, big boy," Jack shouted to the giant as he disappeared behind them on the horizon. "You'll be seeing me again, very soon!"

• • •

As the magic carpet coasted up the driveway, it was barely six inches off the ground and had lost all of its kick. When the group finally stepped off of it, the beautiful little rug dropped to the ground and rolled itself up, just as it had been delivered to the girls. Daphne leaned over and picked it up gingerly, the way one would a tired kitten, and cradled it in her arms.

"Poor thing is all worn out," she said, cooing.

Sabrina looked toward the forest. Hamstead's squad cars were still perched in the tall trees behind the house, but he and his men were nowhere to be seen. Reaching into her pocket, Sabrina removed Granny Relda's enormous key ring and began the tedious job of unlocking all the bolts. Jack watched attentively until she had unlocked every one. Before Sabrina could say the magic words that gained them entrance, Daphne pulled her aside, cupped her hand over her big sister's ear, and whispered, "Should we let him in?"

It was a fair question. Every time they had broken one of Granny Relda's rules they had regretted it, but they were in a tough situation. Jack was probably the only person in the world who could confront a giant, and he had offered to help.

"I don't think we have much of a choice," Sabrina whispered back. She made a fist and knocked on the door. "We're home."

Jack cocked an eyebrow in confusion.

"Family tradition," Sabrina said in hopes of throwing him off. "Granny does it and it makes Daphne laugh so I picked it up, too."

Daphne faked a laugh.

Jack shrugged. "Whatever."

"What's he doing here?" Puck said as he floated down from the sky.

Jack turned around and eyed the flying boy, whose huge wings flapped hard to allow him to hover over them.

"He's offered to help," Daphne explained, but this time her diplomacy was falling on deaf ears.

"Help us do what, try on some big pants?" Puck sneered, taking a jab at Jack's recent job. "You weren't supposed to bring him back."

"Listen, you little brat, I'm the only hope you've got," Jack replied. "Two little girls and a garden gnome aren't going to stop a giant."

"Who are you calling a garden gnome?" Puck said, pulling his flute from his sweatshirt. "My royal army knows how to deal with insolent peasants."

"Boys!" Sabrina and Daphne cried in unison. "That's enough!"

Puck and Jack backed off. The girls looked at each other. Apparently, there was a bit of Granny in them both.

"What happened to Hamstead and his deputies?" Sabrina asked.

"Charming came by and picked them up," Puck said, staring

a hole into Jack. "I sat up on the roof and watched him scream at them for half an hour. It was hilarious."

"Good, we could use a break," Sabrina said, turning and opening the front door.

Elvis rushed past her and into the kitchen, returning a moment later with Granny Relda's handbag. He dropped it at the girls' feet and began to snarl at it. The girls ignored him. Daphne headed into the living room, set the carpet tenderly on the floor, and plopped down, exhausted, into a chair. She pulled a book out from underneath the cushion she was sitting on and tossed it aside.

"So, this is the famous Grimm house," Jack said as he wandered from room to room, lifting up photographs and snooping around. "Oh, I wish I had my camera with me. No one will believe I was actually inside."

"Make yourself at home, please," Sabrina said. If Jack heard the sarcasm in her voice, he pretended not to and continued his snooping.

"So girls, where can I take a kip?" he asked.

Daphne looked at Sabrina for a definition but Sabrina shook her head.

"I have no idea what that means."

"You know, hit the sack?" Jack said.

"You want to go take a nap?"

"I'm zonked."

"We didn't break you out of jail so you could camp out in our house."

"Kids, I was on a lumpy jail cot all night. I need to get some rest, and besides, my big plan can't go into effect until tomorrow night, anyway."

"What big plan?"

"Right now, it's best that we don't discuss it." Jack fell onto the couch and stretched his arms behind his head.

"He doesn't have a plan!" Puck snapped.

"Yes, I do!" Jack replied. "We'll talk about it later. I just need a couple of hours of shut-eye." He closed his eyes and drifted off to sleep.

Puck looked at the girls, turned, and stomped outside, slamming the door behind him.

"What do we do now?" Daphne said sleepily.

"I suppose we might as well get some rest, too," Sabrina said, seeing her sister's head bob. She scooped her grandmother's handbag off the floor and set it on the table, then gently urged Daphne out of her chair. Elvis whined at the girls.

Sabrina turned and whispered into the dog's ear, "Elvis, keep an eye on Jack."

The dog's eyes reflected an understanding, and he seated himself like a stone guardian, watching the sleeping man. The two girls went up to their bedroom. It had been a long day.

• • •

Sabrina didn't remember falling asleep, but when she woke up she was still in her clothes and it was already nine o'clock in the morning. She crawled out of bed, leaving her snoring sister alone, and walked down the hallway. She heard a sound from Granny Relda's room and decided to investigate, but when she opened the door, no one was there.

She stepped inside and noticed a framed photo on the old woman's dresser. It was of Granny and Grandpa, hugging happily under an apple tree. As usual, Mr. Canis was standing nearby. His face seemed slightly out of focus and the camera flash had turned his eyes a bright blue color. Sabrina reached into her pocket and pulled out the photo she had found in Granny Relda's handbag. Comparing the two, she found the same odd effect over Mr. Canis. Sabrina was surprised she hadn't noticed it before.

"What are you doing in here?" Puck's voice asked. It startled Sabrina and she dropped both the picture and the framed photo to the ground. Luckily, the glass didn't break.

Sabrina looked around the room, searching for the boy, but didn't see him. "Where are you?"

"Up here, ugly," said Puck.

Sabrina looked up and nearly screamed. A housefly the size of Elvis was sitting upside down on the ceiling above her. But its enormous size wasn't nearly as disturbing as its human head, which had shaggy blond hair, a gold crown, and a mischievous grin. Apparently, Puck had a whole bag of disturbing tricks.

"What are you doing in here?" Sabrina demanded.

"Uh . . . it's the only quiet room in the house," Puck replied. "Besides, I know you and Jack have got your big plans. Wouldn't want to get in the way."

"Could you come down here?"

Puck suddenly morphed back into his human form and fell clumsily to the bed below.

"You're being a baby," Sabrina said. "Jack wants to help, and you can't stand not being the center of attention."

"Whatever," the boy replied. "But when he gets you into trouble, don't be angry when I remind you that I told you so."

"You got a better plan, then let's hear it, 'cause all I've heard from you is the never-ending buzz of your flapping lips," Sabrina snapped. "My parents ran out on me and Daphne almost two years ago. We've been through the wringer and have been bounced around for far too long. I admit, when we met Granny Relda I didn't want anything to do with her. But now that I know she's the real deal, I'm going to do whatever it takes to get her back. I've lost one family. I'm not losing another. So if you have a better idea, then I'm all ears!"

"Don't look at me," Puck said. "I've made no promises to the old lady. She knew I wasn't a good little boy when we met."

Sabrina was taken aback by his insensitivity. "So you couldn't care less what happens to her?"

"I've learned one thing in this life of mine. Look out for yourself. Everyone else will just end up disappointing you."

"So you won't help?"

"I'm not one of the good guys," Puck said.

Suddenly, the sound of Elvis's barking filled the room. Sabrina peered into the hallway. There, she saw Jack fighting with Elvis, who was shredding the man's pants in his angry teeth.

"Get this beast away from me! He's rabid," Jack begged.

"What are you doing up here?" Sabrina asked, suspiciously.

"I was coming up to wake you."

Daphne entered the hallway rubbing sleep from her eyes. "What's going on?"

"The Giant Killer is prowling around the house looking for something to steal," Puck said. "Your savior has sticky fingers."

"Shut your mouth, you dirty little hooligan," Jack shouted.

"It'll take more than your words to make that happen, you thieving barn rat."

"Elvis," Daphne said as she patted the angry dog on the head—her touch seemed to have a calming effect on him—"take a chill pill."

Elvis released Jack's pant leg from his teeth.

"Thank you," Jack said, eyeing his mangled trousers. "So, are you ready to hear my plan?"

Sabrina looked at Puck, hoping the boy might reconsider and help them, but he sneered and looked away.

"Yes, we're ready," she replied.

Puck said nothing. He walked down the stairs and out the door, slamming it behind him.

"We don't need him, anyway," Jack said. "Is anyone hungry? Let's have some breakfast!"

He rushed down the stairs and into the kitchen, the girls following behind. They watched as he rifled through the contents of the refrigerator.

"There's nothing to eat in this house," Jack complained. "I could really go for some bubble and squeak or some bangers. Do you kids think you could cook up some steak-and-kidney pie for me?"

The girls stared.

"I hear noises coming from his mouth but they don't sound like words," Daphne said.

"Maybe he's having some kind of fit," Sabrina said.

Jack rolled his eyes, snatched up some leftovers, and ate greedily.

"Let me tell you kids," he said, his mouth full, "prison food is terrible."

"We'll take your word for it," Sabrina said.

While Jack ate, the girls took turns telling him how Granny Relda and Mr. Canis had been kidnapped. Sabrina told him her theory about Mayor Charming being the mysterious Mr. Englishman, and how she thought he was using the giant to scare people off their land.

"So, tell us your plan," Daphne said as Jack finished his breakfast.

"I'm still working out the details."

Both the girls flashed Jack an angry look.

"Don't worry!" he said defensively. "It's going to be brilliant."

Sabrina had had enough. She got up from her seat and grabbed the telephone.

"We helped you escape from prison so you could help us save our grandmother and all you have done is eat our food and drool on our sofa," she raged. "If you can't do it, then I'm just going to call Deputy Crane and let him know you're ready to go back."

"Put the phone down and relax," Jack said calmly as he helped himself to another chicken leg. "You think tracking down a giant is easy? Giants have survived thousands of years being as big as they are and they've learned a few things about staying out of sight when they need to. Now we can traipse through the woods, cut down the forest, and drag the Hudson River, but the fact is that if a giant doesn't want to be found, he's not going to be found."

"You're talking in circles," Sabrina complained.

"What I'm saying, duck, is that we have to be smarter than a giant to catch a giant. You said it yourself, that the mayor was trying to cover up what happened to that farm. It's no secret he wants to buy up the entire town. What better way than to get a giant to scare off the landowners who won't sell? So when your family started snooping around, he sent the big boy after you. He's got your granny and now he's after the two of you. All the evidence you need was chasing us down Main Street yesterday."

"Go on," Sabrina said, as she set the phone back in its cradle.

"Knowing Charming, he's got a map of Ferryport Landing in his office, with all the property he's after and where he's going to send the giant next. All you have to do is sneak into his office during the ball tonight, find the map, and see where the giant's next target is. Then we show up, the giant shows up, I do what I do, and bingo-bango, we kill the big boy and save your grandmum."

"That's your big plan?" Sabrina cried.

"You got something better? I know that sneaking into the ball doesn't sound as exciting as burning down the forest and waiting for the giant to run out, but I've always had a mind that tells me the easiest way is the best way."

"There's one big problem, though," Daphne spoke up. "The mayor and the police are looking for us. We're going to have a tough time sneaking into the place."

"Oh, girls, you're going to go right through the front door and no one is even going to notice," Jack said confidently.

After he had eaten, he insisted the best way to digest a meal was to follow it with another kip. As their "hero" rested, the girls frantically searched the books for anything that might help. Eventually, they came upon one of their grandfather Basil's many journals. Inside, he had sketched out a rough plan of Charming's estate.

The mayor's mansion was a sprawling several-story palace with dozens of rooms. Their grandpa had given estimates of room sizes, locations of various windows, and even an indication of a wall he believed held a secret door. But Grandpa hadn't seen all of the house, and many parts of the drawing were labeled with question marks. Sabrina noticed he had paid extra attention to possible escape routes—apparently, Grandpa had been a bit of a sneak as well.

Sabrina carefully studied the map and did her best to commit it to memory. When Jack finally woke up, several hours later, he found the girls ready to get started.

"The first thing we need is the magic mirror," Jack said.

"I don't know what you're talking about," Sabrina said, stealing a look into Daphne's eyes.

"Girls, I know Relda has the magic mirror. Everyone knows that. Why do you think the front door has a dozen locks on it?"

Sabrina took the keys out of her pocket and led her sister and their guest up the steps. Once they arrived at the mirror's room, she inserted the key and unlocked the door. As before, the face in the mirror was filled with rage at the invasion.

"WHO DARES?" he bellowed.

Jack strolled in without a care, followed by the girls.

"Turn off the drama, Mirror," he scoffed.

"Oh, it's you," Mirror mumbled.

"Of course it's me. I'm the bloke you call when you have a big problem, and these girls have a really big problem," Jack bragged.

"And where is the carpet?" the face in the mirror asked Sabrina.

"Sorry," she said. She walked to the doorway and called for it. After a couple of minutes, the carpet floated limply into the room.

"What have you done to it?" Mirror cried as the carpet fell to the floor and once again rolled itself up.

"I think we had too many people on it," Daphne explained as a hand broke the surface of the mirror and snatched the carpet from the ground.

"It's nearly unraveling in my hand," the face wailed as he babied the rug. "Poor little carpet, look at how they treated you."

"Too many years hanging on a wall in the Grimm house have made you a real sourpuss," Jack commented.

"How can I help you?" Mirror asked, brushing off the insult.

"We need to sneak into Charming's mansion tonight and we need some disguises," Jack said.

"Not a problem at all."

"And we need the slippers."

Mirror frowned. "Absolutely not," he stammered.

"Listen, this house is going to be surrounded with the police any minute now. Ali Baba's carpet isn't going to get us into Charming's mansion. We need the slippers," Jack argued.

"Mrs. Grimm would not approve. The slippers were entrusted to this family so they would never fall into the wrong hands," Mirror replied.

"You can trust me," said Jack.

"Didn't you used to have your own magic items? What happened to the Cloak of Darkness?"

"I lost it in a game of poker."

"You lost a cloak that turns you invisible in a poker game? What about the Shoes of Swiftness?"

"I hocked them."

"The Cap of Knowledge? The Goose that Laid the Golden Egg?"

"Lost the cap in a game of dice. And I accidentally left the window open one day and the goose flew off."

"I suppose you sold the Sword of Sharpness?" Mirror grumbled.

"No, I still have the Sword of Sharpness," said Jack indignantly. "I just misplaced it. It's in my flat somewhere. The point is, we need the slippers. If you won't let me have them, then let one of the girls wear the shoes. It doesn't make any difference to me."

"What slippers?" Sabrina shouted. She was tired of their bickering.

"Dorothy's slippers," Jack and Mirror shouted.

"Dorothy from *The Wizard of Oz*?" Daphne exclaimed.

"Yes," Jack said impatiently. "They can transport you anywhere you want to go, all you have to do is . . ."

"Click three times!" Daphne cried. "Gimme the slippers!"

"Girls, I have to warn you. The slippers are very powerful magic. People have died trying to get them. There are still those . . . some in this town . . . who would slit your throats to possess them," Mirror said.

"Enough of this," Jack said, and then he did something that shocked Sabrina. He stepped into the reflection and pushed the man in the mirror aside.

"How dare you!" Mirror shouted.

"C'mon kids, keep up!" Jack said as his face appeared in the reflection.

The girls were unsure of what to do. Daphne reached up and curled her hand into her sister's. Sabrina squeezed softly and the two of them took a tentative step through the mirror. It was a cool sensation, almost as if they had been caught in a summer rainstorm, and when they finally opened their eyes, a brilliant glimmering light flooded their pupils. What they saw made Sabrina queasy. It wasn't natural. It just wasn't possible.

Sabrina had expected to walk into a reflection of the room they had been in. After all, the mirror was a mirror. But she couldn't have been more wrong. Instead she found herself in a long, wide hallway that reminded her of Grand Central Station. It was vast, with a vaulted ceiling and endless archways of glass and steel. Glowing marble columns held up the ceiling, which rose hundreds of feet above them. Breathtaking sculptures of men and monsters lined the hall. And along each wall were hundreds of doors of all shapes and sizes, some no bigger than a rabbit, others a hundred feet high. Some were wooden, others steel, and still others seemed to be made from pure light. Sabrina looked down at Granny Relda's key ring and realized what all the keys were for. Yet another of Granny's eccentricities had a legitimate explanation.

Even more startling than the gigantic room they were standing in was the man who lived in it. The face in the mirror was no longer a disembodied head, but a short, chubby little man in a black suit and tie.

"Keep your hands in your pockets, Jack," the man insisted.

"Mirror, I am shocked. Don't you trust me?" Jack said.

"I trust you about as much as the person who gave you that fat lip," said Mirror.

"What is this place?" Daphne asked.

"It's an arcane-powered, multi-phasic, trans-dimensional pocket universe," Mirror replied.

"A what-who?"

"Your grandmother calls it the world's biggest walk-in closet." The little man sighed. "It's a sort of holding area for dangerous and valuable items. I call it the Hall of Wonders, and you're not supposed to be in here."

"Oh, Mirror," Jack said. "We've learned one of your secrets. Don't worry, I'm sure you have a million more."

The little man's face flushed with anger. His fists clenched and he looked as if he might hit Jack, but the giant killer just ignored him.

"All right, Mirror, where are the slippers?" Jack asked impatiently.

"This way," Mirror said, gesturing for them to follow. He walked down the long hall past many doors. The plaque on one read FAIRY GODMOTHER WANDS while the next read TALKING PLANTS. As they continued down the hallway, they found more doors labeled: POISONOUS FRUITS, DRAGON EGGS, IMPOSSIBLE ANIMALS, WISHING WELLS, CRYSTAL BALLS, CURSED TREASURE, SCROLLS AND PROPHESIES, and on and on and on. Passing one massive door, the group jumped as violent pounding from within threatened to knock it off its hinges. Something on the other side wanted out, something named GRENDEL.

The group pressed on down the hallway where they finally stopped at a door that read MAGIC SHOES.

"Here we are," Mirror said reluctantly. "But I must once again remind you that magic is dangerous. There's a reason why the Everafters asked this family to look after all of these things. Magic in the wrong hands only leads to chaos."

"We'll be careful," said Sabrina as she knelt down to the lock. It was a simple one that would take a skeleton key, but Granny's key ring had dozens of skeleton keys. Sabrina tried the first one and it failed. She tried another; still nothing.

"Let me try," Jack said impatiently.

"I've got it," Sabrina snapped. She turned another key, and this time the lock opened. The door swung wide and everyone entered.

The room was simple, but its contents were amazing. Along the walls were hundreds of pairs of shoes: cowboy boots, woven sandals, wooden clogs, leather moccasins, and many more, all displayed on wooden shelves. Some of the shoes seemed as if they had been made for animals, while others were big enough for the entire group to stand in. One golden pair had downy, white wings that flapped as if the shoes were alive, and another glittering pair were made of pure glass.

Jack picked up the pair of shoes with wings, but the little man promptly smacked his hand and snatched them from his grip. After replacing the shoes, Mirror crossed the room, picked up a pair of sparkling silver slippers, and handed them to Sabrina.

"Try to take better care of these than you did the magic carpet," he said gruffly.

If these were the famous ruby slippers, they were more silver than red, though in the light Sabrina saw hints of a warm, rosy color. She couldn't figure out what they were made of, but if forced to guess, she would say they were tinfoil.

"Put them on, child," the little man said.

"They're way too small," Sabrina said as she eyed the shoes.

"One size fits all, duck," Jack said.

Sabrina yanked off her sneakers and slid her foot inside one of the slippers, which magically grew in size and fit her foot perfectly. Once she had the other one on, an odd energy crept up her legs and filled her whole body.

Just then, Jack darted out of the room and across the hall.

"Jack!" the little man shouted after him, but Jack didn't listen. When they finally found him, the giant killer was eyeing a door with a plaque that read MAGIC BEANS.

"I can't believe you have a whole room of them!" he shouted with glee.

"We might be bending the rules on the slippers, but those are off-limits to the likes of you!" Mirror said.

"How about a peek?" Jack pleaded. He suddenly looked like a lost little boy. "These things are part of my past. Can't a man take a walk down memory lane?"

Sabrina could see his expression, and all at once she felt sorry for him. Jack was a man whom the whole world had loved. He had seen amazing things and lived life to the fullest, but being trapped in Ferryport Landing had put an end to all of it. It dawned on Sabrina that Ferryport Landing might have been the home of many of the world's fairy-tale creatures, but it was also a prison they were never allowed to leave. It didn't seem right.

Sabrina pulled out the keys, knelt down, eyed the keyhole, and within seconds opened the door. Jack pushed past her into the tiny room, where a single mason jar sat on a table. Inside it was a collection of little white beans.

Jack gasped and picked up the jar. "There must be a hundred of them."

Mirror snatched the jar out of his hand and placed it back on the table.

"These things are dangerous. If you dropped them on the floor we'd be ear-deep in giants."

Jack scowled for a moment and looked as if he were ready to fight for his treasure, but he took a deep breath and his anger vanished, only to be replaced with a boyish grin.

"Thanks, Grimms, you don't know what you've done for me," he said.

Mirror hurried everyone back through the door.

"Well, ladies, now that we've got the shoes, we need the proper disguises," Jack said. "I think a little fairy godmother magic will do the trick."

"Wands are over here," Mirror said, leading them down the hallway. They stopped at the door labeled FAIRY GODMOTHER WANDS and Sabrina unlocked it. Inside, a small black cauldron sat on a tiny table, with several skinny sticks popping out of the top. Mirror reached into the pot and removed one that had a glittery glass star on the end, and handed it to Sabrina.

"The first magical item your family ever had to confiscate," Mirror said.

"I remember old Wilhelm Grimm trying to get that away from her." Jack laughed. "Girls, I'll say one thing about your family. They are brave. Fairy godmothers are sweet as pie on the outside, but try to take away their wands and they can get downright mean."

"Indeed," Mirror said.

"How does this work?" Sabrina asked.

Mirror frowned. "I can't believe your father!" he cried. "I'd hoped that your mother, Veronica, might at least give you the basics behind his back. Very well, this is the changing wand used by Cinderella's fairy godmother. It will alter your clothes, shoes, even your bodies, in any way you want."

"Charming's ball is going to be filled to the rafters with Everafters," Jack said. "You're going to go in as one of them."

Daphne smiled. "I know what I want to be! I want to be the Tin Woodsman!"

"Are you sure, honey?" the little man in the mirror asked. "Tin is so last season."

Daphne nodded enthusiastically.

"Very well, it's your fashion funeral," he said. "Sabrina, just say 'Tin Woodsman,' make three small circles with the wand, and then tap her on the head."

"OK," Sabrina said. "Tin Woodsman!" She made three awkward circles in the air and then smacked her sister on the head with the wand. Daphne squealed in pain and rubbed the spot, but as she was rubbing, a miraculous change began to occur. Her skin took on a silvery tone. She grew several feet taller and her clothes faded, only to be replaced by gears and joints. Her hair retreated into her scalp and a shiny funnel took its place. Sabrina blinked her eyes to be sure they weren't playing tricks on her, but she knew they weren't. Her sister had become the Tin Woodsman.

"That hurt," Daphne cried as her hand scraped against her new metallic head. Hearing the screech of metal in her ears, she looked at her hand and squealed in delight. She walked around the hall, squeaking with every step. "Look at me!"

"Spitting image," Jack said.

Daphne took the wand from her sister. "OK, who do you want to be?"

Sabrina was stumped. She realized she had to choose wisely. She needed to be inconspicuous at the ball, someone small and unnoticeable, and someone who could be very, very sneaky.

"OK, I was thinking . . ."

"I know, Momma Bear!" the little girl interrupted and before Sabrina could stop her, she had performed the circles and was cracking her big sister on the head.

Sabrina felt the transformation immediately, as if her body was being inflated. Her clothes disappeared and were replaced with a bright, pink-and-white polka-dotted dress that ended well above her knee. She looked down at her humongous arms and groaned as hair exploded from every pore. Fangs burst from the top of her mouth and razor-sharp claws sprang from her fingernails and toenails. She could feel them scratching at the insides of the ruby slippers, which had expanded to fit her new size-twenty-six feet. When the transformation was complete, Daphne giggled.

"You did that on purpose!" Sabrina growled.

"You are so cute!" Daphne cried as she threw her metal arms around her sister and gave her a big hug. "I could just eat you!"

"Well, no one's going to see the two of you coming," Jack moaned, though it was obvious he found the whole thing funny.

"Girls, you realize there's a timer with this magic. When the clock strikes nine o'clock, you're going to change back. Do you understand?" Mirror lectured.

"Nine o'clock? I thought it was midnight. Cinderella had until midnight," Sabrina argued.

"Cinderella was seventeen years old. You are eleven. There's no way your grandmother would approve of you staying out until the wee hours of the morning."

"We're trying to save her life," Sabrina pointed out.

"Still, children should not be allowed out that late, thus, your magic wears off at nine," Mirror said.

"That doesn't give us much time, it's seven o'clock right now," Jack said, eyeing his wristwatch.

Mirror took the wand from Daphne and put it back into the pot. He led the group out of the room, closed the door, and, when Sabrina couldn't manage, locked it with Granny's keys.

"One last thing," Jack said. "You don't happen to have any walkie-talkies in this place, do you?"

9

hen the group stepped back through the mirror, Sabrina suddenly felt her massive size. Being a seven-foot-tall, twelve-hundred-pound grizzly bear made the regular-sized room feel much smaller.

"I'll never get through the doorway," Sabrina worried.

"You won't have to," Jack said as he stepped through the reflection. "Just click those heels together and you'll go anywhere you want. But before you do, you'll need these."

Jack held three walkie-talkies. He opened Sabrina's handbag and stuffed one inside, then slid open a panel in Daphne's tin frame and popped in the other. He kept the third for himself.

"These will help you keep in touch with me."

"You're not going in with us?" Sabrina asked.

"Are you kidding?" Jack cried. "I'm on Ferryport Landing's

'Most Wanted' list by now. Even if I disguised myself, Charming is sure to have security that can sniff me out. I can't take the chance. I'm going to stand outside the mansion and direct you. When you find the map of Charming's next target, we'll go save your grandmother and Canis."

"OK," Sabrina said, looking down at the slippers on her huge, furry feet. "I just click them together?" she asked, feeling ridiculous.

"Three times," Daphne cheerfully reminded her.

"There's no place like Charming's mansion?"

Jack nodded in agreement. Daphne put her hand on Sabrina's arm and held on tightly. Jack reached over and did the same.

"There's no place like Charming's mansion. There's no place like Charming's mansion. There's no place like Charming's mansion."

The last thing Sabrina saw was Elvis trotting into the room. In his mouth he had the piece of fabric Granny claimed was from a giant's pants, as well as a big scrap of Jack's pants. He spit them out on the floor and whined for attention, but suddenly there was a pop and the lights went out. Sabrina's ears filled with a squeaky sound, like someone was slowly releasing the air from a balloon, and when the lights came back on, the three of them were standing in front of Charming's estate.

It was the biggest house Sabrina had ever seen, with several stories and marble columns like the ones on the White House framing a golden front door. A coat of arms depicting a lion fighting a snake decorated the front of the house. The lawn was immaculately trimmed and bordered by stone paths and clipped shrubbery. A statue of Prince Charming surrounded by admiring woodland animals rose out of a fountain in the middle of the lawn. Several hulking attendants with green skin and oversized muscles—parking valets—waited by the circular driveway, opening car doors, taking keys, and driving the cars away.

A car pulled up in front of the house and a blond woman in a blue bonnet and puffy dress got out. She reached into the backseat for a long white staff with a curled end. Before the attendant could close the door for her, half a dozen lambs tumbled out and eagerly followed the woman inside.

"Little Bo Peep," Daphne cried. "Can you believe it?"

"OK, girls, I'm going to stay out here and let you know if the cops show up. Keep your radios on and try to stay inconspicuous," Jack said.

"I'm a grizzly bear in a dress," Sabrina muttered.

"Charming's office is on the second floor," Jack continued. "I'd mingle with the guests for a while, work the crowd, and find your way up there without attracting attention."

"Oh, is it that easy?" Sabrina said.

"Once you find the map, pop yourselves back down here and we'll go find your giant," Jack finished. He gave them a thumbs-up sign and disappeared into some nearby trees.

"He makes it sound so simple," Sabrina grumbled to Daphne.

A line had formed as guests waited to be announced, so the girls walked to the back of it. In front of them were a large man and his wife, having some kind of argument.

"Isn't there a line for the rich people?" the woman groaned.

"Maybe if we had gotten here earlier we'd be inside already," the man grunted. His voice was slurred and Sabrina thought he might be drunk.

"I wanted to look nice for the ball," the woman said defensively.

"You wanted to look nice for the prince," he muttered.

"Are you going to harp on that, again?" The woman sighed. She turned and noticed Sabrina and Daphne. Her cheeks flushed red and she forced a sheepish smile to her face. Even in her embarrassment, the woman was radiant. Her beautiful amber hair cascaded in curls down her neck and her bright-green eyes sparkled in the light, competing for brilliance with her pearly white smile.

"Good evening," she said politely.

Her husband turned to see who she was speaking to, and the agony of his face was revealed. His features were pushed flat, giving him a cat-like appearance, accentuated by the mane of hair that framed his face. Long fangs crept out of his mouth and hung down nearly to his chin. But his most horrible feature was his eyes, bright-yellow slits that blinked at them fiercely. Sabrina knew exactly who they were—Beauty and the Beast.

"Good evening," the Beast grunted. "Nice to see you, Woodsman. How on Earth did you and Momma Bear come to be acquainted?"

The girls weren't prepared for questions and stood dumbfounded.

"You're such a gossip," Beauty scolded. "What Poppa Bear doesn't know won't hurt him."

Several more guests joined the line. Sabrina turned around to see a small white rabbit in a vest clutching an old-fashioned chain watch in his paw. He looked at the time and stuffed the watch back into his vest pocket.

"For once, we are not late." The White Rabbit sighed with relief. His companions were three mice wearing black sunglasses and carrying canes.

"Always the worrywart," one of the mice said as he tapped his cane against the ground.

"I told you we would make it," the second added.

"Someday I'd like to smash that watch of yours. All that worrying about time is going to give you a heart attack," the third mouse concluded.

"I believe in being punctual," the White Rabbit said defensively.

"Have you heard the news?" the second mouse squeaked to the crowd.

"No, I want to tell. I heard it first," the first mouse cried. "Relda Grimm has been carried off by a giant!"

The folks in line gasped in surprise and turned their attention to the little mouse.

"Are you sure?" the Beast asked.

"Maybe you'd prefer an eyewitness," the first mouse cried. "I may be blind, but my hearing is just fine."

The Beast rolled his eyes.

"A giant? That's impossible," Beauty exclaimed.

"I didn't believe it, either, but it's true," the White Rabbit replied. "The giant has been stomping around all over town scaring the humans to death. The Three are working overtime, showering the town in forgetful dust. Be prepared to dig deep, my friends. The damage is extensive and forgetful dust costs a pretty penny. You all know Charming's going to ask us to foot the bill."

Sabrina hung on every word.

"If she's dead, we might actually be able to leave Ferryport Landing!" Beauty cried, unable to hide her excitement. "Has anyone tried?"

"The barrier is still intact," said the third mouse, almost stumbling over a pebble as he stepped forward with the moving line. "We tried it this morning."

"Well, I wouldn't get your hopes up about Relda meeting an untimely demise," the White Rabbit said. "I'm sure Canis will save her. He always does."

"Oh, that's not going to be a problem this time," the third mouse chirped. "The giant carried him away, too!"

"Two birds with one very big stone," the second mouse sang with glee.

"So, it's just a matter of time," the Beast said.

"Maybe not," the second mouse said. "I hear they've found the granddaughters."

Everyone groaned.

"I thought they had died!" Beauty said.

"No, just missing. Apparently, whatever carried off their parents didn't get them," the White Rabbit said.

"I'm sorry," Sabrina interrupted. "But did you say the girls' parents had been carried away?"

"The family thinks they abandoned them, but I've heard whispers that Henry and his wife were kidnapped," the Beast answered.

Sabrina and Daphne shared a stunned look.

"But it's not all bad news," the first mouse said.

"Indeed?" Beauty asked.

"I hear they're already trying to rescue their grandmother. Can you believe it?" said the White Rabbit. "Two kids taking on a giant! The whole family will be pushing up daisies by morning."

"That's the dumbest thing I've ever heard, and when it comes to the Grimms, that's saying something," the Beast said.

The crowd laughed.

"Momma Bear, you must be so excited," Beauty said, taking Sabrina's heavy paws into her delicate hands. "Soon, you'll be reunited with your family. Are they still hiding out in that Romanian zoo?"

"Uh . . . yes, that will be wonderful," Sabrina muttered, doing her best not to swat Beauty across the yard and then stomp the rest of them into paste. The talk of her parents had caught her attention.

"Do you know who kidnapped the parents?" said Sabrina.

"Who cares?" the White Rabbit replied.

"You people are horrible," a voice said from behind them.

Sabrina turned around and saw a beautiful, dark-skinned woman with dazzling green eyes. She wore a diamond tiara and a beautiful evening gown. She looked at the group in front of her with disgust.

"Briar Rose," Beauty said nervously. "I think you may have stepped into the middle of a conversation and misheard something."

"I heard all I need to hear," Briar Rose said.

The crowd shifted uncomfortably and turned away from her accusing stare while Sabrina's mind filled with possibilities. Could it be true? Their parents hadn't abandoned them? Could someone have kidnapped them?

Soon, Sabrina and Daphne were almost at the front of the line. Mr. Seven stood at the door, this time without his pointy "idiot" hat. He announced Beauty and the Beast and the couple disappeared into the chattering party inside.

"Good evening," Mr. Seven said as he opened the door for them. He cupped his hands together and yelled, "Momma Bear, escorted this evening by the Tin Woodsman," as the girls entered the room.

The mansion was a spectacular display of wealth and taste. A crystal chandelier hung from the ceiling and a beautiful red-carpeted staircase led up to a large landing, where four men played violins. The room was already crowded with people, animals, and monsters of all shapes and sizes—Everafters as far as the eye could see. They wandered around, talking and drinking champagne. Some laughed at jokes while others argued politics. A very ugly couple of trolls dressed in evening wear danced to the music, and several hulking waiters hurried around the room, extending trays of appetizers to guests. No one seemed to be bothered that there were ogres and winged people hobnobbing with talking animals, so Sabrina's worries that people would notice a man made of metal and a bear in a polka-dotted dress quickly dissolved.

"Sabrina, all of the Everafters wish we were dead," Daphne said.

Sabrina looked around the room. Every fairy-tale creature she had ever read about seemed to be here: Cinderella and her fairy godmother, the Mad Hatter, Mowgli and Baloo. Even Gepetto was off in a corner chatting with Ali Baba. And Sabrina knew they all hated the Grimms. As unsettling as it was, Sabrina could understand why. Even though Ms. Smirt had dumped the girls into some awful foster homes, Sabrina and Daphne knew they could always run away. For the Everafters there was no escape, and it had been that way for almost two hundred years. *It must be torment for them,* she thought.

"Where should we start?" Daphne asked.

They needed to get into the mayor's office, but they also needed to know where Charming was while they were doing it. Sabrina looked around the room, but he wasn't present.

"Let's just stay out of the way and keep our ears open. Once we know where he is, we'll make our way upstairs. For now, let's mingle."

The two walked awkwardly around the main room, gawking at the various literary celebrities and capturing bits of conversations.

"So she's not coming?" a dwarf said to a huge black panther. The panther licked its paw and hungrily eyed Sabrina.

"She never comes," the panther said. "If I left him at the altar, the last place I'd want to go is the man's house. I think it's very respectful of Snow White not to show her face here."

"But it was almost four hundred years ago. The man has been married at least half a dozen times since," the dwarf said. "Cinderella, Sleeping Beauty, and Rapunzel are all here. If they can move on, then Snow White surely can. This community is important."

"Ladies and gentlemen, we're pleased that you could attend the Ferryport Landing one hundredth annual community ball," Mr. Seven shouted from the top of the red staircase. The musicians laid down their instruments and everyone turned their attention to the mayor's assistant. "Allow me to introduce your host for this evening. Your mayor, his majesty, Prince Charming."

The violinists immediately broke into a stately song as a pair of double doors at the top of the stairs swung open. The crowd burst into applause as Charming waved and descended the staircase.

He was all smiles, shaking hands with everyone he met, kissing women on the hands, even if they were ugly witches or even uglier stepsisters, and calling everyone by name as he glided around the room. Mr. Seven followed closely behind him, handing out business cards.

"What do you say, Woodsman?" Charming asked, taking Daphne's hand and shaking it vigorously.

"Hello," Daphne seethed, unable to hide her contempt.

Charming reached over, took Sabrina's massive hairy paw, and placed a kiss on it.

"Momma Bear, as lovely as ever," he said with a wink. "I hope the two of you are having a wonderful time."

"We are, thank you," Sabrina said sharply. Maybe she had acquired some of the bear's aggressiveness along with its body, because for the second time that night she thought she might like to swat someone with her paw. One quick swipe and she could probably take Charming's head clean off his shoulders.

Instead, she smiled and did her best to curtsy, imagining how ridiculous this move looked from a twelve-hundred-pound bear.

"Please eat, drink, have a wonderful time. This celebration is for us," Charming said as he swept on to the center of the room.

"Friends, I am so happy that you could all attend the annual ball," he continued. "Each year we gather together as a community to toast our hard work and, most importantly, our patience."

Charming's words sent a frustrated rumble through the crowd.

"But once again, your support is needed to continue to build our community," he said. "There is still work to be done and we need your help to maintain services, to fund our fine police force, and various other community endeavors. So, I ask you, when you contribute tonight, give deeply. In fact, give until it hurts, or I'll put you all in jail!"

For a moment there was complete silence, and then, a broad, boyish grin sprang to Charming's face. The crowd burst into nervous laughter.

Suddenly, a woman pushed through the crowd. Her face was white with powder, as was the long wig she wore on her head. She had used a black pencil to accentuate her eyebrows and lips, and had drawn a large black mole on her left cheek. She wore a royal gown, decorated with large red hearts, and next to her stood two armed guards who, much to the girls' amazement, were playing cards.

"Prince, what are you doing about the giant?" the woman demanded.

The crowd grew silent but Charming merely smiled at her.

"Your majesty, it is such an honor to have the Queen of Hearts here at the gala," he said.

"You haven't answered my question," the queen snapped, eyeing the crowd to make sure all were paying attention. "I think the community deserves to know what you are doing to protect this town and if the money we give each year at this party of yours is well spent."

"Every Everafter can rest assured that my administration is on top of the problem," the prince said. "The sheriff and his deputies have been searching the forests and I have my best witches busy casting locator spells. And if that doesn't work, well, I'll just go lock up the next two-hundred-foot man I see."

The crowd chuckled at his joke.

"That's all fine and good, Charming," the queen replied. "But one must ask how a giant got loose in the first place. This kind of thing would never have happened in Wonderland. When I was ruler, people knew better than to try such shenanigans. You have to be firm with the criminal element."

Some of the crowd muttered in agreement, but Charming only smiled wider.

"Well, Queen, let's not go losing our heads over this," he said. The crowd roared with laughter, causing the Queen of Hearts to turn red with rage. "It's just one giant, and . . ."

"I've heard a rumor that you are actually controlling this giant," Sabrina said, hardly believing the words came from her mouth.

"Momma Bear, I never pegged you for a gossip," the prince replied. "Did this nasty little rumor you heard carry more information? For instance, why I would want a giant smashing up the town?"

"So you could buy the land back cheap and rebuild your kingdom," Sabrina replied.

Charming's face turned pale. "Nonsense," he muttered.

"What if the Grimms hear of this?" said the Queen of Hearts.

"Relda is already aware of it. The giant has carried her off," the prince informed her.

The crowd roared in shock.

"Relda Grimm is in the hands of a giant?" the queen cried.

"As is Mr. Canis," Charming added.

The crowd was silent and then a spattering of applause broke out. Many of the Everafters shook hands and patted one another on the back, while others looked worried and upset.

"Canis will finally get what's coming to him," a troll cheered.

"Take that back!" Daphne screamed. Sabrina tried to pinch her to be quiet, but her paws slid off her sister's tin body.

"People, unfortunately, this celebration is turning into a town hall meeting," Charming called above the noise. "If you have any further concerns I want you to know that my door is always open . . . between the hours of eight and eight fifteen every morning. Please call for an appointment. For now, let's dance, drink, be merry, and most of all, be ourselves, free of the disguises we all wear to fit into this pathetic, boring little town. The night is young, and by the grace of magic, so are we."

Charming's words were followed by another lively tune from the violinists and the festive mood soon returned.

The girls mingled in the crowd, barely able to contain themselves whenever they heard angry, threatening words about their family from the mouths of characters they had grown up loving. It seemed that the only topic of conversation tonight was how wonderful the world would be if the Grimm family dropped off the face of the Earth. When the clock struck 8:45, both girls had heard enough. It was high time they made their move.

"I have to get upstairs," Sabrina said to Daphne. "If we stick around here any longer we're going to change back, and these people will probably kill us. Find somewhere out of the way and warn me on the walkie-talkie if Charming is coming."

"Good luck," Daphne said, wrapping her hard metal arms around Sabrina and hugging her.

Sabrina navigated through the crowd. As she approached the steps, she thought she'd finally found her opportunity. That was until Sheriff Hamstead stepped in her way.

"Young lady, you are under arrest," Hamstead said.

Sabrina wondered what she should do. She could probably knock the sheriff down with one swing of her big bear paw, but everyone would see. Running away didn't seem like an option, either.

"For being the prettiest lady at the ball," the sheriff continued.

"Uh, thank you," she stammered, somewhat confused.

"Wonderful party, don't you think?" said Hamstead as he transformed to his true pig self.

"Yes," she said. "Could you excuse me? I have to visit the ladies' room."

Hamstead apologized and let her pass. Sabrina lumbered up the stairs until she reached the top. She walked past the violinists and down a long hallway. Once she was out of sight of the crowd, she made sure no one was following, then reached into her purse and pulled out the walkie-talkie, awkwardly switching it on with her big paws.

"Jack, I'm upstairs," she said.

"Good job, duck. His office is the last one—" Jack said, his voice popping and crackling.

"I can barely hear you. Say again," Sabrina said.

"It's the last one on the right!" Jack repeated, still sounding distant.

Sabrina walked down the hallway. When she got to the end, she found the door Jack had spoken of. She opened it, and standing before her was another seven-foot grizzly bear ready to pounce. Sabrina screamed, but the bear did nothing. In fact, it didn't even twitch. Sabrina realized it was stuffed.

The room was dedicated to Prince Charming's hunting trophies. Several mounted deer heads, a stuffed fox, and a wild boar overlooked Charming's immense desk. A rattlesnake sat on top of it, poised and ready to strike. What portions of the walls weren't covered in dead animals were hung with portraits of the prince done in various artistic styles. There was even an abstract portrait in which his nose was on his forehead.

"Creepy," Sabrina whispered to herself. She reached for her walkie-talkie and pushed the button again. "I'm in."

"The coast is clear down here," Daphne's voice said. "Charming is busy talking to a raccoon in a tuxedo. That's so crazy!"

"Look for a map or something like that," Jack's voice squawked through the box. "Charming keeps records of everything."

Dozens of files and reports littered the top of the mayor's desk, including an unfolded map of the town. Someone had circled areas in red and written "reported sightings" next to them.

"Jack, are you there?" Sabrina said into the walkie-talkie.

"Yes," his voice crackled.

"I found a map with some circles on it, but there's nothing that says the exact time or location of a meeting. In fact, to me it looks like Charming's trying to track the giant as well."

"I doubt it . . . that . . . homes . . . too." Jack's voice broke up.

"Jack, I can't hear you. Try to get closer," Sabrina said, but there was no response.

"Daphne, I've lost Jack somehow. I'm going to take the map. What is Charming doing?" Sabrina asked.

But there was no response from her sister, either. Sabrina looked around the room. In the corner was a television. Hooked to the back by wires was a video camera, and on the television's screen was a frozen image of the Applebee farm. Sabrina crossed the room and found the remote control. She picked it up awkwardly and after several difficult seconds managed to get her giant paw to press the Play button.

The screen came to life with the most amazing scene. A giant beanstalk was exploding upward from the ground, soaring high into the sky and disappearing off the top edge of the TV. Within seconds, an enormous body came crawling down it and the sight sent shivers through Sabrina. It was the giant she had met the day before. It stomped down on the little Applebee farmhouse just as Mr. Applebee leaped out the door. Granny had been right. The lens cap did mean someone—Charming—had taped the whole violent episode!

"Daphne, I found a tape in Charming's office that shows the giant destroying the farmhouse. Now we have proof that he and the giant are working together," Sabrina said.

But before she could finish her sentence, the door burst open and the Tin Woodsman was pushed inside. Behind her was Charming, looking murderous. He slammed the door and took a crossbow from the wall, where it was hanging like a piece of art.

"I'm sorry," Daphne apologized. "He snuck up on me before I could warn you."

"Who are you?" he demanded.

"I'm Momma Bear," Sabrina lied.

"Is that so?" Charming sneered. "That would be interesting, since it's almost December and you should be three weeks into your hibernation by now."

"I didn't want to miss such a lovely party," Sabrina stammered.

Next to the door sat a quill of arrows. Charming selected one, inserted it in the crossbow, and pulled the bowstring back. Then he aimed it at Sabrina's heart.

"I'm going to give you until the count of five to tell me who you are or your head is going to join the others on my wall," he threatened coolly.

10

’m not playing any more games with you people,” Charming said. “I’ve told you already I’m not interested in joining the Scarlet Hand. Your revolution is not for me.”

“We don’t know what you’re talking about,” Daphne cried.

“One,” Charming began counting.

Sabrina looked over at the clock. There were only seconds left before the magic would wear off, but more than the five Charming had promised them.

“We’re Relda Grimm’s granddaughters,” she blurted out desperately.

“Two.”

“We used a magic wand to change our shape so we could

sneak into your house," Daphne cried. Oily tears leaked from her eyes.

"Three."

"We're not part of any revolution!" Sabrina begged. "We just want our grandmother back!"

"Four."

"We're not lying to you!" Daphne sobbed.

"Five."

Sabrina closed her eyes tightly and awaited her death, wondering if she would be stuffed like the other bear in Charming's office or if her body would change back after her heart had stopped beating. But when nothing happened, after a few more moments, Sabrina bravely opened her eyes. She and her sister had magically transformed back into their normal states. The only evidence of their disguises was the oily smears on Daphne's cheeks.

"Ladies, I could toss you into jail and throw away the key for what you've done," Charming said, removing the arrow from his crossbow. "You've used a magical item to help a known criminal escape from jail, infiltrated an Everafters party without an invitation, impersonated Everafters, committed espionage against a government official, broken into my home, put the Ferryport Landing Ball in serious jeopardy, and ruined two pairs of Sheriff Hamstead's pants."

"We didn't ruin your stupid party," Sabrina argued.

"If that crowd downstairs sees the two of you here, the top of this house will fly off," Charming replied. "The only way we're going to prevent a mob is to have Hamstead toss you in some old sacks and carry you out the servants' entrance. He can take you down to the jailhouse and let you cool off in a cell."

Sabrina lunged for the video camera. The wires came with it and the image of the giant faded from the television screen.

"We're not going anywhere without our grandmother and Mr. Canis," Sabrina said. "This tape is all the evidence we'll need. How do you think those people downstairs are going to feel knowing you intend to buy up this town and smash any-one that gets in your way?"

Sabrina expected Charming to fight for the tape, but instead he only laughed.

"You are just like your parents." Charming chuckled. "Henry was always shooting his mouth off before his brain could catch up and Veronica was the suspicious one. What an unsettling combination you are."

Suddenly, something moved in the window. Sabrina turned her head, but nothing was there. "Did you see that?"

"See what?" Charming asked as a giant, puss-filled eye peered into the house.

"ENGLISHMAN!" a booming voice growled, shaking the windows in their frames.

"That!" the girls shouted.

Charming calmly picked up the phone on his desk and dialed a number. "Mr. Seven, are you aware that there is a giant outside?" he said into the receiver, as if he were informing a waiter that there was a hair in his soup. "Oh, you didn't know. Well, now you do . . . No, this isn't some kind of emergency drill . . . Well, I agree, we should do something about it before the guests panic. Maybe you should send the witches out to put a protection spell on the house . . . Well, of course it's a good idea!"

Charming slammed the phone down, crossed the room, and dragged both girls roughly out of the office and down the hall.

"Where are you taking us?" Sabrina demanded.

"Keep your heads down and don't say a word," the prince sneered. "I'm taking you outside."

An acidy fear rose up in Sabrina's throat as they stumbled out of his office and into the second-floor hallway. "You can't take us out there with that thing!" Sabrina cried, pulling at Charming's vise-like grasp.

"You wanted to find your grandmother. Well, her ride just showed up," he said.

"HELP!" Sabrina cried as they turned a corner and headed

down a long hall toward the back of the house. Daphne took her sister's cue and called for help as well, causing many of the guests to look up and see what was happening.

"Those are the Grimm children!" an orangutan shouted angrily.

"No need to let it ruin your evening," said Charming, with his toothy smile. "I have the situation under control."

"They're spying on us!" the Queen of Hearts gasped. "Off with their . . ."

"They aren't spies, my friends," the prince said as he changed course and pulled the girls down the stairs with him into the angry crowd. "Please, go back to the celebration."

But before he could get the words out of his mouth a horrible crunching sound filled the room. The partygoers looked to the ceiling, only to see it ripped away right before their eyes. Pieces of plaster fell down around everyone and a collective scream erupted among the Everafters.

"The sky is falling! The sky is falling!" a chicken cried as it raced for the door, only to get caught in a stampede of terror when the hole in the roof was replaced by the giant's horrible, gnarled face, breathing its rancid, rotten-egg breath down on the crowd.

The Queen of Hearts ran to a nearby window, threw open the curtains, and tried to climb out. Her playing card attendants rushed over in time to catch her from falling over. The rest of the crowd ran in all directions, and the panic gave Sabrina and Daphne a chance to break Charming's grip. They rushed into the crowd and ducked between legs and feathers as all sorts of unusual creatures rushed around them.

"Where is the murderer?" the giant bellowed.

"He's not here, big boy. The murderer is not here," Charming shouted as he turned to face the monster.

"Liars! You protect him," the giant growled. "I smell his murderous blood. He released me only in hopes of killing me but my fate will not be like that of my brothers and sisters. He is here and I will have him."

Charming looked up the staircase to the violinists, who were scattered in fear. "I didn't tell you to stop playing," he said, snapping his fingers at them. Bewildered, the musicians went back to their overturned chairs, set them upright, and began playing music as if a giant wasn't staring down at them.

"Fe, fi, fo, fum, I smell the blood of an . . ."

"I think we've all had enough of your temper tantrum," Charming interrupted. Suddenly, three figures fluttered into the air and hovered around the giant's head. One of them was an ugly old woman darting through the air on a broom; the second was a strikingly exotic beauty dressed all in black, who levitated off the ground; and the third was a blond lady inside a silver bubble. As she floated by, Sabrina recognized her as Glinda from the hospital. All three had magic wands that they waved threateningly at the giant. The monster swatted at the witches, but they weaved and bobbed out of the way of his massive hand. The ugly witch waved her wand and a rocket of flame shot out of it and exploded on the giant's chest, searing his shirt and causing him to scream in agony.

"Stop!" Daphne cried. "Our family is in his pocket!" The little girl broke away from her sister and ran outside. Sabrina, followed by Charming, rushed after her.

The witches had flown out of the hole in the roof and now continued their assault.

"Leave while you can, Giant!" Charming shouted.

The second witch raised her wand and a stream of lightning fired out of it, hitting the giant in his face. The giant roared with pain and raised his hands to block the bolt. A charred, black smear was added to the other ugly features on his grizzled face.

Glinda waved her wand and a spray of ice froze the giant's backside and continued to cover the rest of his body. Within seconds, the massive man was encased in an ice tomb, but soon cracks appeared and, with flexing muscles and a powerful roar, the giant broke free. Enormous chunks of ice rained down on the parking lot, flattening an unlucky car.

The doors of the mansion were thrown wide and a dozen men rushed out past the girls. Each was in a purple tunic embroidered with a red lion on the chest. Swinging their swords wildly in the air, they roared a war cry as they rushed toward the giant. At the front of the attack was a man Sabrina instinctively knew to be King Arthur. The knights charged the giant's feet, and together they whacked angrily at an exposed big toe. The giant roared at the assault and stomped his feet angrily, trying to squash his attackers. Each of the men was lightning quick and dodged the giant's blows, managing to strike at his exposed ankle in the process. Shrieking in pain, the giant quickly turned and fled.

Charming knelt in respect as the king and his knights turned to face him.

"I am indebted to the Knights of the Round Table. Thank you, Your Highness," Charming said.

"Your thanks will not be enough, Charming," King Arthur barked. "The beast destroyed my car. Trust that you will find a repair estimate in the mail this week."

Charming scowled, but as the party guests filed out of the half-destroyed mansion, he forced a smile. Mr. Seven rushed to the prince's side, carrying a large black pot he held out to the approaching crowd. "Friends, who says nothing exciting ever happens in Ferryport Landing?" The prince chuckled. But this time his wit and charm fell on angry ears. The people passed him, returning his laughter with disgusted looks.

"Is this what we're paying you for?" the White Rabbit said as he hopped past.

"People, there's no need to leave," Charming said. "We'll have the mansion back to its old self in just a matter of moments. There's plenty of food and drink and we've even arranged a door prize."

"As the elected leader of this community, I would have thought you'd take the safety of your constituents much more seriously," a Bengal tiger said as he stalked past them.

"I assure you, Shere Khan . . ." But the tiger didn't stop to hear Charming's assurances.

"Well, if you all must go, please don't forget to donate to the Ferryport Community Fund," the prince continued, kicking Mr. Seven, who immediately held the pot higher so that everyone could see. But not a single penny was added to the donations.

"I do believe this town is in need of some new leadership," the Queen of Hearts said, as she left. Charming said nothing as he watched the last of his guests drive away.

"Put the pot down, Mr. Seven," he said. The dwarf slowly lowered the empty pot and took a peek inside.

"We want our grandmother and her friend," Sabrina demanded.

"This is all your fault!" Charming shouted as he turned on them.

"What?"

"You two brought him here."

"If you can't control your giant, then maybe you shouldn't be working with one," Daphne advised.

"I'm not working with any giant. Only a fool who wants to be someone's lunch would make a deal with a giant," Charming said.

"That's a lie," Sabrina yelled. "He's one of your goons, just like those guys you met at the cabin."

"Ladies, I am nobility. I don't have goons. Those men don't work for me. I was there to arrest them and their boss."

"Well, if you're not their boss, who is?" Sabrina demanded.

Charming snatched the video camera from Sabrina's hand. He opened a side panel where a small LCD screen folded out. Then he rewound the recording, pressed the Play button, and handed the camera back to the girls.

The image was shaky at first but then suddenly it cleared up as the person holding the camera set it down on the hill that overlooked Applebee's farm. Four men were talking to one another.

Two of them were extremely tall, another was short and fat, and the fourth couldn't be seen. It was obvious who the other three were—Bobby, Tony, and Steve—the goons who had attacked the family at the hospital. Finally, the fourth figure stepped in front of the lens, leaned down, and grinned broadly. It was Jack.

"That's evidence we found on Jack when he was arrested. He wanted a tape of himself killing a giant," Charming cried. "It had nothing to do with the farmhouse. In fact, he admitted he thought the farmer had left town."

Jack laughed wildly at the camera, held up a small white bean, and then rushed down the hill. Soon, the familiar footage of the beanstalk and the destruction of the giant played again.

"So, you're not trying to buy up the town to rebuild your kingdom?" Daphne asked.

"On the contrary, I *am* trying to buy up this town," Charming said. "But there are better ways to get what you want than to let a giant loose on the countryside."

Sabrina didn't know whether to be furious with his admission or respect his honesty.

"So why did you send the sheriff after us?" Daphne asked.

"He was supposed to pick you up and take you somewhere safe until we could hunt down the giant and find your grandmother," Charming said.

"Every Everafter in this town wishes we were dead," Sabrina said. "Why would you want to help us?"

"I have my reasons."

"I'm confused," Daphne said. "Why would Jack bring us here and tell us this story about you being the bad guy?"

"And why did he want to stay in contact with these, if he was just going to take off?" Sabrina said, handing Charming her walkie-talkie.

"Because, if he kept you busy he could go back to your house," the prince said.

"But he can't get in. He doesn't have the keys," Sabrina replied.

"He doesn't need the keys," Daphne gasped. "We didn't say 'good-bye' to the house when we left. We used the ruby slippers. The house is unlocked."

Hamstead, in his human form, came rushing out of the mansion.

"I've got the deputies chasing the giant," he said. "He's heading into the woods in the direction of Widow's Peak."

"Good job," Charming said. The sheriff beamed with pride.

"We've also searched the grounds. There's no sign of Jack," Hamstead continued. "But we did find this."

He held out Jack's bloody handkerchief.

"So the giant would smell him and come running," Charming said. "You might as well join your men, Sheriff. The girls and I will call you if we need you."

"Where are you going?" Hamstead asked.

The prince took Sabrina's arm and urged Daphne to do the same. "We're going back to the Grimm house. I have an unsettling notion of what our giant killer is up to," Charming said.

Sabrina clicked her heels together.

"There's no place like home. There's no place like home. There's no place like home."

Instantly, the girls and Charming were standing outside of Granny's house. The front door was wide open and through the doorway they could see that Jack had ransacked their home. They walked inside. Bookshelves were tipped over, furniture was overturned, and even the couch cushions were thrown aside. He had searched through every kitchen cupboard, emptied closets, and destroyed antiques. But his crimes against the house weren't what was bothering Sabrina. What hurt her was that she had been tricked. In the last year and a half, Sabrina had learned to be street-smart and savvy. She was the one who was supposed to pull fast ones on people. She was the queen of the sneaks and she had been suckered.

Suddenly, the telephone rang. She picked up the receiver and said hello.

"Hello, this is Wilma Faye at Action Four News. I'm following up on a tip we got about a half hour ago. A Mr. Englishman said there would be a murder on Widow's Peak tonight. We've already got a camera crew on their way but we were hoping we might be able to speak to Mr. Englishman first," the woman begged.

"No, he's not here," Sabrina replied.

"Well, if you see him please tell him that we are very intrigued by the story and will have a camera team and reporter there as he requested," the woman continued. Then, with a click, she hung up.

"That was a reporter," Sabrina said. "Jack called them and told them there was going to be a murder on Widow's Peak tonight."

"This is exactly what I was trying to prevent. He's going to kill a giant on television so he can be famous again," Charming said. "When the world sees that, this little town will be turned upside down by reporters. There's too much here to explain. We've got to stop him."

"Elvis!" Daphne cried suddenly. The giant dog was nowhere to be seen. Daphne shouted his name and, after several painful moments of silence, a low bark could be heard from upstairs.

Daphne rushed up the steps, followed by Sabrina and Charming. She threw open the door to Mirror's room and found Elvis lying on the floor in a small puddle of his own blood. He had a serious cut on his belly but he barked happily when he saw the girls. Daphne knelt down and kissed the dog gently on his nose. When she lifted her face, tears were pouring down her cheeks.

"He hurt Elvis," the little girl sobbed.

"Girls, we have to find Jack," Charming said coldly. "We don't have time for this mongrel."

Sabrina and Daphne looked at the man as if he were a moldy sandwich that had slowly turned to soup in the bottom of the refrigerator. The prince groaned and took his cell phone from his pocket. He dialed a number and sighed impatiently.

"Mr. Seven, I need you to send one of the Three to the Grimm house. The door is open so they can come right in. There's a dog that needs medical assistance . . . Yes, a dog . . . a D-O-G. No, Mr. Seven, I don't know what's wrong with him, maybe a broken rib . . . No, Mr. Seven . . . Yes, Mr. Seven . . . Mr. Seven, if you don't stop asking me questions, I'm going to feed you to this dog."

Sabrina eyed the man suspiciously and Charming caught her gaze.

"And Mr. Seven, my orders are that whichever one of the

witches comes, she respect this house," Charming added. "No snooping."

Daphne wrapped her arms around the prince's neck and hugged him as he hung up his phone.

"Thank you," she sobbed and, for a brief moment, Charming seemed to enjoy the hug, but then he pulled away from her.

"You're ruining my suit," he replied, wiping his lapel clean of the girl's tears. "We should check the mirror."

Sabrina gazed over at it. The little man who was usually in its reflection was missing.

"Mirror!" Charming shouted.

"You have to step through it," said Sabrina.

"I'm aware of how it works," the prince said impatiently. "I used to be engaged to one of its former owners."

He stepped into the reflection and disappeared. Sabrina followed closely behind, leaving Daphne to nurse Elvis.

The little man known as Mirror was lying on his side on the cold marble floor, barely conscious and covered in bruises. Charming knelt down to him and lifted the pudgy man's head. Mirror slowly opened his eyes and grimaced in pain.

"He was too strong and fast for me. I couldn't stop him," Mirror groaned.

"What did he take?" Charming asked.

"I tried to fight him off but he just laughed at me. You wouldn't believe how quick he is," Mirror complained.

"Focus, man! We need to know if Jack took anything."

"He took the beans," Mirror replied.

"How? He doesn't have a key," Sabrina asked, reaching into her pocket and pulling out Granny's key ring.

"I forgot to remind you to lock the door after you let him take a peek at the jar," said the little man.

"I don't get it," Sabrina said. "If killing the giant will make him famous again, what does he want with the beans?"

"It's insurance. If his fame starts to fade, he'll let another giant out with another one of those beans. The giant will kill people and destroy things and then Jack will come to the rescue," Charming explained.

"But how is he going to find the giant in the first place?" Sabrina asked. "We haven't been able to find him and he's two hundred feet tall."

"He's not going to have to find it, it's going to find him," Charming answered. "Giants have a great sense of smell, especially when it comes to blood. That's why the giant showed up at the mansion. Jack left his bloody handkerchief and the giant could smell it. It's amazing, really, that they can smell anything over their own stink. If one touches you, you can't wash off the odor for weeks."

Suddenly, Sabrina thought of the two pieces of fabric Elvis had brought into the room just before the group had left for Charming's mansion. One was Granny Relda's cloth from the giant, the other was a piece of Jack's pants. *Elvis was trying to warn us that Jack had been near a giant,* Sabrina realized. She was a terrible detective—she couldn't recognize a clue when it was offered to her by a two-hundred-pound Great Dane. She wanted to kick herself, but she had to focus on what Charming had said.

"But if giants have such great noses, why didn't this one attack us here? Jack was in our house for hours," she said to Charming.

"Protection spells. If Relda is anything, she's careful. We have one on the jailhouse, too," he replied.

"So, what are we going to do?"

"Mirror, I'm going to need something," Charming said.

• • •

Sabrina unlocked the door labeled MAGICAL ARMORY and let the prince inside. The room was filled with all types of weapons—bows and arrows, swords, a nasty-looking pole with a spiky metal ball attached by a chain, and hundreds of others. Some things were obviously magical, as they glowed or hummed, while most were just shining with horrible possibilities.

Charming pointed to a sword on the wall. "That's the one," he said.

Mirror hobbled into the room with a worried face. "I find this very unwise. There is already one Everafter running around with magic; this town does not need a second. Especially with Excalibur. Any person whose skin is pierced by its blade is a goner. Even the tiniest scratch will kill you."

Sabrina took the sword off the wall and held it in her hand. It was long and wide, with a jewel-encrusted handle. An odd tingle raced through her when she held it with both hands. She felt powerful, the way King Arthur must have felt when Excalibur belonged to him.

"Sabrina, is this someone you can trust?" Mirror asked.

"No, he's not," she said. "I've heard what this town thinks of my family and what my death might mean for your freedom. How do I know you won't just stab me in the back when I'm not looking?"

"Grimm, I am not your friend," Charming said. "I resent your family for the life they have forced me to live for the last two hundred years and I resent you for the future that you represent. And if I were doing this for your worthless family, you would probably be right. But I'm not doing this for you. I'm doing it for me. As much as Baba Yaga's spell has trapped me in Ferryport Landing, it has also benefited me. I have power here. I have wealth and respect. If Jack shows the world that giants and fairy tales are real, then life in this town will change and my position as its ruler . . . I mean mayor, might be challenged. Therefore, you and I are in an unusual situation. Tonight, I am your ally, and I will help you save your grandmother and Canis. If that is the only solution, then so be it. But rest assured, Grimm, tomorrow I am your enemy again."

Sabrina looked up into his eyes and saw that he was being honest, even if his brand of honesty made her sick to her stomach. Could she trust him? She reached into her pocket, took out the picture of her family, and gazed at their faces—her mother and father, Mr. Canis, and finally, Granny Relda. She had to do something to get the old woman back. She wasn't going to lose her family all over again. She took the heavy sword and handed it to him.

Mirror continued to protest, limping along, as Charming and Sabrina exited the room and returned through the mirror. Daphne was waiting for them with Elvis. They gently carried the dog into the hallway and then Sabrina carefully locked the door to Mirror's room.

"You stay here with Elvis," Sabrina ordered her sister.

"No way!" Daphne cried. "We're Grimms, this is what *we* do!"

"This is dangerous."

"Whatever," the little girl said, grabbing Sabrina's hand tightly.

Sabrina surrendered, hooked her finger into Charming's pocket, and clicked Dorothy's shoes together.

"There's no place like where Jack is," she said.

"Sabrina, wouldn't these shoes take us to wherever Mom and Dad are?" Daphne wondered aloud. Sabrina's eyes grew wide with possibility.

"We can save them next," her sister said happily.

"All right," Sabrina said, clicking her heels together. "There's no place like where Jack is. There's no place like where Jack is."

The lights went out and the familiar squeaky wheeze filled Sabrina's ears. In a split-second, Charming and the girls were standing in the woods on Widow's Peak. They had little time to adjust to their new surroundings. Sabrina looked above her and saw the giant's massive foot preparing to crush them all.

They managed to leap out of the way but the aftershock tossed them around as if they were on a sinking ship. The ground split apart, sending stones and soil into a gaping crevice where the group had once stood.

The giant leaned down to get a better look at the three people scurrying at his feet. He reached to snatch them, but a flaming arrow zipped from the tree line and landed in the side of the giant's face. The monster cried in pain as he plucked it from his cheek, only to have a second and third arrow pierce his chin.

"Stop it, Jack!" Sabrina commanded. "There are people in the giant's pocket and if you kill him they'll die when he falls!"

Jack peeked his head out from behind some branches in a nearby tree and laughed.

"Oh, it's not time to kill him yet," Jack shouted, remaining safely hidden in the trees. "I'm just trying to get him good and angry."

"We know about the reporters, Jack," Charming said. "We're never going to let that happen."

Jack fired several more arrows into the giant's face, landing a painful shot to the monster's lower lip. The giant raged as he tried to pluck it out. While the giant was busy, the young man dropped out of the tree and landed as nimbly as a cat.

"Blimey! Charming and the Grimms on the same side? I never thought I'd live to see the day," he said. "Has the prince turned traitor like that worthless mongrel Canis?"

"The only allegiance I have is to myself," Charming said as he waved Excalibur in the air. "Now, we can do this the easy way or the hard way. But the result will be the same. You're going back to jail."

"Sorry, Prince, but I've spent my last day in the Ferryport Landing lockup. My fans await," Jack said, loading another arrow into his bow and firing it at the giant. It pierced the skin between two fingers of the giant's left hand, and he shrieked. Overcome with rage, the giant swept his arm across the tops of the forest trees, cracking many ancient cedars in half. A sizable chunk of one fell from the sky and nearly hit Charming in the head.

"Oh, he's angry now." the giant killer laughed, loading his arrow again. This time he aimed it at Charming.

"Jack, don't!" Sabrina cried.

"I was hoping it wouldn't have to come to this," he said as he lined up his arrow with Charming's heart. "But don't worry. I promise to have them spell your name correctly in your obituary."

He released his arrow and the girls watched it soar through the air at Charming. Daphne screamed and squeezed her sister's hand, knowing Jack's aim was true. But something happened the girls didn't expect. Charming lifted Excalibur slightly and the arrow bounced off its metal blade and fell to the ground. Jack was flabbergasted.

"What luck you have!" he cried.

"Try again and see if it was luck," the prince said, stepping forward with the sword.

With hands like lightning, Jack fired another arrow and Charming deflected it with similar results. Jack pulled three arrows from his quill and lined them up together on his bow. He fired them all at the same time. Sabrina watched in amazement as Charming guided Excalibur to block each from their deadly course.

"I can do this all night," the prince bragged, but just then the giant's monstrous hand swung down and hit him from behind. Excalibur was knocked free of his grip and fell at Sabrina's feet. Charming was sent sailing through the forest, landing painfully against a tree and slumping to the ground.

Jack pulled more arrows from his quill, lit them with a lighter Sabrina recognized from Granny's kitchen, and fired five off with furious speed. Each landed in more of the giant's sensitive spots. The painful barrage was enough to get the giant to back off, giving the young man an opportunity to turn on the girls. He put another arrow into his bow and aimed it at Sabrina.

Instinctively, Sabrina reached down and snatched Excalibur from the ground. It was incredibly heavy and bulky but she swung it around in the air the best she could.

"And what do you think you're going to do with that, duck?"

Jack scoffed as he stepped toward her. "Grimms aren't killers. You don't have it in you!"

"Well, we're kind of new at this job. If we break a couple of rules, that just goes with the learning process," Sabrina said with as much bravery as she could muster. Her courage was short-lived. As Jack got closer, she noticed something painted on his shirt. It was a red hand, just like the one the police had found in her parent's abandoned car. It sent a chill through her body.

"You took my parents," Sabrina said.

Jack looked down at the red hand and smiled. "No, girl, I didn't, but I know who did. The Scarlet Hand has plans for them."

"Where are they?" Daphne cried.

He laughed.

"You know, I grew up reading about you," Sabrina said, trying to keep him busy. "You had a very exciting story. You climbed the beanstalk, killed the giant, and captured the treasure. Lots of kids think of you as a hero."

"But not you?"

"Once, but not now. Now that I've met you—the real Jack—I see what a rotten person you are. That's what you're famous for now, Jack. Not being a giant killer, but being scum."

"Give me the sword, girl, so I can cut your tongue out with it," he threatened.

"Daphne, I want you to run away and get some help," Sabrina said. She knew she couldn't deflect Jack's arrow and didn't want her sister to see her die.

"I won't do it," Daphne insisted.

Jack pulled his bowstring back further and, just as he was about to fire his arrow, the giant's foot came down on top of him, giving the man only a split second to leap out of the way.

Daphne grabbed her sister's hand and together they raced into the forest, dodging trees and branches. Jack followed closely behind, and worse, the giant strode after him. Its first step landed several yards behind them.

An arrow whizzed by and impaled itself into a nearby tree.

"That was a warning shot, ladies," the young man shouted as he loaded another arrow. "I'm quite good with this thing."

Suddenly, the two girls were slipping down the side of a hill and into an ice-cold creek. Another arrow splashed in the water at Sabrina's feet as they pulled themselves out of the stream and continued to run. With now-frozen feet, they did their best to avoid the jagged rocks that littered the forest floor, but soon Sabrina took a tumble and fell end-over-end across the ground.

She tried to stand up and quickly realized she was missing something—her left shoe—Dorothy's left slipper—lay glistening in the moonlight behind her. It had fallen off.

"C'mon," Daphne begged as she tried to help her big sister to her feet, but Sabrina crawled desperately toward the shoe. It was their only chance of finding their parents. She used her arms to pull herself along the ground, knowing that Jack would fall upon her at any second. But before she could reach it, the giant's foot came down hard on top of the slipper. The vibrations shook the girls and sent them tumbling. When the giant lifted his foot, the shoe was gone; the only thing remaining was a piece of glistening fabric that turned to dust in Sabrina's outstretched hands.

Heartbroken, Sabrina pulled her sister behind a huge oak tree and the two of them rested.

"Don't worry, I'll think of something," she said, squeezing her sister's hand.

But the sound of a monstrous crash drowned Sabrina's answer and flooded the forest. Splintering wood and damp soil rained from the sky as the tree they stood next to was violently uprooted.

The two girls looked up into the face of death towering above them and felt its hot, pungent breath blow their hair back from their scalps. *What's happened to our lives?* Sabrina wondered.

The giant tossed the tree aside and then reached down with his grubby hand to pick them up, but just as he did, Sabrina thrust Excalibur into the air. The giant's hand plunged into its blade, and suddenly his eyes lit up in surprise.

"What was that?" he asked softly. He stood up as if he was in a daze, unsure even of where he was. The anger in his face melted away, replaced by a sort of calm curiosity, and he began to wobble on his feet. Unable to keep his balance, he sailed backward, landing flat on his back and crushing an acre of forest beneath him. A thick cloud of dust rose above his body and settled down all around them. Half a pound of soil landed in Sabrina's blond hair.

And then, all was still.

"I didn't mean for that to happen," Sabrina said, looking in horror at the sword still clutched in her hand.

"Granny Relda and Mr. Canis?" Daphne whispered as tears filled her eyes.

Jack rushed through the brush and saw the giant, lying dead on the ground.

"You've killed him," he said angrily. "*I* was going to kill him!"

"It's over, Jack," Sabrina said.

"It's not over until I say it is," Jack raged. "I'm going to be famous again, but for another reason. Tonight, the Everafters of Ferryport Landing are going to find they are suddenly free from the spell that has kept them in this mercilessly boring town for two centuries. With your grandmum now dead, the spell turns to the last living Grimm. Some might be patient enough to wait for you two to die of old age, but I am not. This ends tonight."

11

ack rushed forward and violently shoved Sabrina to the ground. Daphne lunged at him, but she received the same treatment. Sabrina had dropped Excalibur in the fall and Jack quickly picked it up, admiring its blade for a moment and then readying himself to bring it down on Sabrina's head.

"They're going to have a parade in my honor for this," the young man said with a sick smile.

Suddenly, a loud, wheezing honk filled the night. Jack spun around. In the giant's breast pocket, a wonderful thing appeared: Two headlights blinked to life. An engine roared, backfired violently, and then, with a squeal of tires, the family car ripped through the pocket and sped along the giant's body. At the wheel was Mr. Canis and, next to him, Granny Relda, safe and sound. The car soared over the giant's gelatinous belly, down his leg, and hit his huge kneecap, sending the car sailing into the air. It landed several yards away from Jack and the girls and skidded to a stop. The engine puttered out, the lights went dim, and the car doors opened. Granny Relda stepped out with a very concerned face.

"Jack, what is the meaning of this?" she asked.

The young man pulled the mason jar of beans out of his jacket and held it up.

"It's about this, old woman. It's about capturing my rightful place in the spotlight," Jack said.

"Those days are over," Mr. Canis said, as he stepped out of the car.

"Maybe for you, traitor," Jack snarled. "But I've got bigger plans than selling shoes and measuring hemlines. These beans are going to make me a hero again. But for that to happen, some things have to change around here."

"What are you suggesting?" Granny Relda asked.

"The Grimms have to die."

"You know I won't allow that, Jack," Mr. Canis said.

"I've been killing giants since I was a lad. I suspect I won't have too much trouble with an old mutt like you."

Mr. Canis looked over to Granny Relda. Something passed

between them—a sort of question and answer that only the two of them shared. Granny Relda nodded in approval and Mr. Canis took off his hat.

"If you want to sic your dog on me, Grimm, then do it. But I'll have my destiny either way," Jack said, putting the jar of beans back into his jacket and swinging Excalibur around menacingly. "I've been waiting for this for a very long time."

Mr. Canis smiled in a way Sabrina could only describe as eager. Once again, she was sure he was doomed. The old man had managed to take out three overweight goons, but could he handle a lightning-fast slayer of giants carrying a sword that killed anything it touched?

Jack charged wildly, screaming into the air, but before he could even swing the deadly sword, a change came over Mr. Canis. His shirt ripped off his chest as his body doubled in size. His feet snapped and stretched as they transformed into paws. Hair sprang from every inch of skin, fangs crept down over his lips, his nose extended out, replaced by a snarling snout, and the tops of his ears twisted into points and raised to the top of his head. But most disturbing were his eyes, as they changed into an achingly bright blue color. The same color Canis's eyes were in the picture Sabrina had found of her family. The transformation was complete. Mr. Canis had turned into a wolf the size of a rhinoceros.

"Bring it on, little man," the Wolf snarled, as it jumped up on its back legs. Sabrina could hear a hint of Mr. Canis's voice in the Wolf's growl, but the way he said the words held nothing of her grandmother's feeble old friend's calm. The Wolf's voice was full of viciousness.

The Wolf charged at Jack and sent him hurtling backward into a tree, giving the young man no time to recover as the Wolf savagely sunk its teeth into Jack's right arm. Jack screamed in agony. With the Wolf on top of him, he couldn't swing the deadly sword. The best he could do was hit the beast on the head with Excalibur's handle. The Wolf backed away, slightly dazed, and then licked its lips.

"Bad news for you, Jack," the Wolf barked. "I know your taste now, and I like it."

In the commotion, Granny held out her arms for the girls and they ran to her side.

"Everything will be fine," Granny consoled them.

"You didn't tell us Mr. Canis was one of them," Sabrina said.

"Oh, didn't I? Yes, Mr. Canis is the Big Bad Wolf," Granny said as she kept her eyes on the fight.

"The Big Bad Wolf?" the girls cried.

The Wolf lunged at Jack, ripping his chest with its razor-sharp claws. Jack swung back and punched the beast in the

face, but the Wolf just chuckled. Desperately, the young man jumped up, grabbed a tree branch, and used it to catapult himself at the Wolf. The force sent them both tumbling over each other, leaving Jack on top.

"When I kill you, this town is going to erect a statue in my honor," Jack boasted. "How does it feel to know that your own kind wish you dead?"

"Not nearly as bad as it must feel to know they don't care if you are alive," the Wolf snarled as it rolled over on top of Jack. "Maybe they'll notice when I leave your rotting corpse hanging in the town square. That is, after I've eaten all the juicy parts."

Jack thrust his knee into the Wolf's belly, knocking the wind out of it, and giving the young man the chance to throw the beast off. He crawled to his feet and picked up Excalibur.

"Even the tiniest scratch will send you on your way, mongrel," Jack warned. He rushed forward, pushed the beast against a tree, and held the lethal blade to its neck. "Perhaps they will now call me Jack the Legend Killer, as well."

Sabrina looked to her grandmother and saw the worry in her face. She knew Jack was going to win, and then he would turn on them. How would the three of them fight him off? But suddenly, above the snarling and fighting, she heard an odd sound, as if someone had just played some notes on a flute. At first,

Sabrina thought she might have imagined it, but then a swarm of pixies darted out of the woods and surrounded Jack. He cried in pain with every little sting and soon blood began to leak from all over his body.

"No one likes a bragger," Puck said as he floated down from the trees and rested on a branch above the fighting.

"Puck!" Daphne cried. "You really are a hero!"

"Hush, you'll ruin my reputation," Puck replied.

In vain, Jack tried to brush the pixies off, swatting at them wildly with little result and dropping the sword in his struggle.

"Old lady, are you well?" Puck asked as he floated to the ground. "I tried to tell Sabrina that Jack couldn't be trusted but she wouldn't listen. She's very stubborn and stupid."

"I'm sure Sabrina had her reasons, Puck," Granny replied as she winked at her granddaughter. "But before we can celebrate, Jack has a jar in his coat we need."

Puck smiled, took out his flute, and played a quick, sharp note. One lone pixie left the others and buzzed around the boy's head.

"We need to get that jar away from him," Puck said. The little light blinked as if to say yes, and zipped into the storm of pixies tormenting Jack. Suddenly, a small group of them flew into his jacket and collectively carried the jar of magic beans away.

"No!" Jack cried in panic, swatting and swinging wildly at the pixies. Seeing his prize carried off, he desperately grasped for the jar, only managing to knock it to the ground, sending shards of glass and beans in all directions.

"Oh, dear," Granny gasped.

The Wolf fell over as if it was having a fight with itself.

"I'm not going back inside, old man!" the beast bellowed. It groaned and complained as it transformed back into Mr. Canis. The old man was exhausted and broken. He had a worried look on his face.

"We have to get the children out of here," Mr. Canis gasped.

Suddenly, the Action Four News van came careening through the woods and stopped. The doors slid open and Wilma Faye got out, followed by her cameraman. The reporter fixed her business suit, checked her hair in a small compact mirror, and then turned to face the girls.

"Girls, I'm Wilma Faye from Action Four News. We heard there was a story out here tonight," the woman said, but her words were drowned out by a horrible rumbling. The little white beans were taking root. They dug deep into the forest's soil and instantly a hundred little green sprouts popped out of the ground. The sprouts grew at an alarming rate, becoming vines and then stalks that jockeyed among one other for space.

They soared higher and higher into the air until it seemed they would touch the moon itself.

The cameraman tapped Wilma Faye on the shoulder and the reporter turned around.

"What is it?" she said impatiently.

The cameraman pointed up and Wilma's eyes followed. Above her were dozens of angry giants quickly climbing down the beanstalks. The cameraman pointed his camera into the air, flipped a switch, and a bright light mounted on the camera lit up their faces.

"Are you getting this?" Wilma asked, panicking.

"I'm getting it!" the cameraman shouted.

"What have you done?" Jack bellowed.

"You wanted giants, Jack. You're going to get your wish," Granny Relda said, as the first giant planted a foot on the forest floor. Dozens and dozens of them followed, all in all nearly a hundred, knocking over trees that had been growing for centuries. Each one of the giants was uglier than the last and all of them had murder in their eyes.

One of the most gnarled of the bunch stepped forward. It let out an ear-shattering roar and pounded on its chest.

"Fe, fi, fo, fum, I smell the blood of that murderous Englishman!" the giant bellowed at Jack, sending his hair flapping behind him.

"I didn't kill your brother, it was the girl," the young man cried, pointing a shaky finger at Sabrina. "Sabrina Grimm killed him!"

The giants looked down at Sabrina with suspicious eyes. One ducked his head down, shoving it into the girls' faces. His nostrils blasted hot air into their clothes.

"Lies!" the giant bellowed, spraying Sabrina and Daphne with its hot, snotty breath. "These are children. They could not kill one of us!"

As the giant swooped down and grabbed Jack in his huge, grimy hand, Granny Relda stepped forward. "What do you plan on doing with him?" she asked the giant, as if she were talking to an ordinary person.

"Crush his bones to paste and eat him with some bread, Grimm." The giant grunted. "Or maybe we will pull his little limbs off one by one and see if he screams."

"You'll do nothing of the sort," Granny Relda replied. "Take him to your queen. She'll decide what to do with him."

"Help me, Relda!" Jack cried. "Don't let them take me!"

Granny Relda lowered her eyes. "I cannot deny them their justice. I only hope they are more merciful with you than you have been with them."

Jack saw the futility of his words, and calmed himself, then he laughed, almost insanely. "Do you think I did this all on my own?" he ranted. "Where do you think I got the first magic bean? They've got Henry and Veronica. The Scarlet Hand is coming and your days are numbered!"

The giants ignored Jack's threats and turned back toward their beanstalks. A few leaned down and gingerly picked up their dead brother. They carried him on their shoulders as they climbed up the beanstalks and disappeared into the cold night air, just as three squad cars roared into the clearing with lights and sirens going. Flying high above the police were Glinda in her bubble and Hansel and Gretel's Frau Pfefferkuchenhaus on her broom. They sent a stream of fire that lit the bases of the beanstalks, setting them all ablaze.

Hamstead got out of his car and, along with Boarman and Swineheart, rushed to the family's side.

"I hope that you are OK, Relda," Hamstead said.

"Of course, thank you very much, Sheriff," Granny replied.

"You've got some pretty smart grandchildren," Hamstead said, smiling at Puck, Sabrina, and Daphne. "Not ones to let a man explain anything, and not so easy on my wardrobe, but I suppose they're pretty smart."

He reached his hand out and Sabrina shook it. Daphne did the same.

"In the future, kids, remember, we're the good guys," Hamstead said. "If you'll excuse me, I have to confiscate a little evidence."

The sheriff looked at Mr. Canis and nodded his head.

"Wolf," he said with an odd respect.

"Pig," Canis replied, returning the gesture.

Hamstead excused himself again and approached the cameraman and the reporter. He said something to them and they immediately began to argue. The portly sheriff grabbed the camera and tried to remove the videotape inside. He managed to take it out and break it in half, but got several whacks on the head from Wilma Faye's microphone for his efforts.

"What about the reporters?" Daphne asked.

"Glinda will make sure they don't remember a thing," Charming said as he entered the clearing. He was rubbing his head and placing his phone back in his pocket.

Mr. Canis stepped closer to the family as Charming stopped in front of the girls.

"Relda, your grandchildren are as meddlesome as you are," the prince continued. "But they were helpful in putting an end to Jack's plan."

"Your Majesty," Relda chirped happily, "are you suggesting that the Grimms might be useful in this town?"

"Hardly," Charming growled. He turned to the girls and

looked at them darkly. "Remember what I said about tomorrow, children." He spun around and made a beeline for the sheriff.

Daphne and Sabrina hugged their grandmother around the waist and burst into a torrent of happy tears. Granny Relda leaned down and covered the girls in kisses.

"*Lieblings*, are you OK?" she asked.

This time, Sabrina didn't feel like pulling away from the old woman. This time, Granny's hug felt like home.

"I'm OK," Sabrina said, fighting back more tears.

"We're sorry we almost got you killed," Daphne said. "We're not very good detectives."

"Nonsense!" Granny Relda laughed as she led them to the car. "You rescued Mr. Canis and me and managed to prevent a serious catastrophe. I say the two of you are first-rate detectives. We should celebrate. Does anyone have any ideas?"

Sabrina eased back into her seat. "I'd really just like to get out of these clothes," she said, looking down at the monkey hanging from the tree on her sweatshirt.

HANG IN THERE, it read.

• • •

Elvis woke the girls the next morning with loving licks on their faces. Luckily, Jack had not hurt the dog too badly. His ribs were bruised and he would have to wear a bandage on his side until the veterinarian could remove his stitches. But the only thing that seemed to truly hurt was Elvis's pride. Daphne apologized to him for not paying attention to his clue and promised that his opinion would always be considered in the future.

Granny greeted them at the dining room table with more of her unusual culinary treats. That morning, they enjoyed blue scrambled eggs, some little orange nuts, home fried potatoes soaked in sparkly green gravy, and wedges of tomato. Mr. Canis was still in his room and Puck was nowhere in sight.

"Is Mr. Canis OK?" Daphne asked.

"He will be," Granny Relda replied. "I'm sure he'll be happy to hear you are concerned."

"Where's Puck?"

Granny Relda smiled. "He'll be here soon."

After breakfast, the three Grimms went to the mall and bought the girls a dozen outfits apiece. Even Granny found a new hat with a sunflower on it that matched a yellow dress she said she hadn't worn in years. Sabrina suggested they burn their orange monkey sweaters and blue heart-covered pants but Daphne refused. Granny took Sabrina aside and apologized for the outfit, saying that Mr. Canis might not have been the right choice to shop for girls. After all, he was color-blind.

When they got home, Granny had presents for them. The girls unwrapped them quickly and found they each had a brand-new, cloth-bound book, just like the one in which their father had kept his journal. The covers had their names stenciled in gold with the words FAIRY-TALE ACCOUNTS above them. When Sabrina opened hers, she found there was nothing inside, only hundreds of blank pages.

"As your father and generations of Grimms before him did, it is your responsibility to put on paper what you see, so that future generations can know what you went through," Granny said. "We are Grimms. This is what we do."

The rest of the day, the girls scribbled what had happened into the books. They picked each other's brains for anything they might have forgotten and when they were finished, Sabrina tucked the picture of her family inside her journal's pages. Together, the girls rushed downstairs and placed their books alongside their father's on the shelf reserved for their family.

"Girls, I'd like to show you something else," Granny said. The girls followed her up the stairs, where she unlocked Mirror's room. The little man's face was in the glass again and he smiled when the old woman and the girls entered.

"Good afternoon, Relda," Mirror said.

"Good afternoon. I do hope you are feeling better," Granny replied.

"Much better. The bruises look worse than they felt," Mirror said.

"That's nice to know," the old woman said. She turned to the girls and took their hands. "Would you like to see your parents?"

Sabrina's heart nearly jumped from her chest.

"Is it possible?" she asked.

Granny turned back to the mirror. "Mirror, mirror, near and far," she said aloud. "Show us where their parents are."

The mirror misted over and two figures slowly appeared in the reflection. When the mist cleared, Sabrina saw her parents, Henry and Veronica, lying on a bed in a dark room. They were very still, with their eyes closed.

"They're dead," Sabrina said, before she could stop herself.

"No, not dead," Granny Relda corrected her. "Just sleeping."

"We lost one of Dorothy's slippers," Daphne cried. "We could have used them to rescue Mom and Dad."

Sabrina's face flushed with regret.

"*Liebling*, don't you think I have tried the slippers and everything else inside the mirror?" Granny Relda sighed. "This Scarlet Hand, whoever they are, used strong magic to take your

mom and dad away from us, but we aren't going to give up. We'll find them, I promise."

The girls wrapped their arms around Granny Relda and hugged her tightly. Sabrina and Daphne sobbed, both tears of happiness that their parents weren't dead and tears of despair that they didn't know where they were.

"I hope you'll let me into your family until we can all reunite," Granny said, breaking into tears herself.

Suddenly, there was a knock at the downstairs door. The old woman took a handkerchief from her pocket and wiped the girls' eyes. Then she wiped her own and stuffed the hankie back into its home.

"Come girls, we have guests," she said as she exited the room. The girls watched the image of their parents slowly fade from the mirror and then stood for a moment, staring at their own reflections.

"We're home now," Sabrina said to her sister.

"Well, duh!" Daphne giggled.

The two left the room and closed the door behind them. Then they ran down the stairs to the foyer. Puck was already inside, carrying several boxes filled to the top with old toys, junk, and several dead plants. Behind him were Glinda, Hamstead,

Boarman, and Swineheart.

"What are the police doing here?" Sabrina asked.

Glinda, Boarman, and Swineheart walked past them into the dining room and spread a huge roll of papers onto the table. When Sabrina got a closer look, she realized they were blueprints.

"What's all this?" she asked.

"We're putting an addition on your house," Hamstead said as his expression turned to a sly smile. "This house isn't big enough. You need another bedroom right away. Relda asked us for our advice. Before we went into law enforcement, we used to be in construction."

"I'm getting my own room," Sabrina squealed happily. "I haven't had my own room in a year and a half."

Daphne looked insulted and stuck out her tongue.

"Oh, Sabrina, we're not building you your own bedroom, yet," Granny apologized. "No, we need another room because . . ."

"I'm moving in!" Puck interrupted. He shoved his box of junk into Sabrina's hands and joined the witch and the deputies looking over the plans.

"He's lying, right?" Sabrina said hopefully. "You wouldn't let that stinky freak move in here with us?"

"I think it's great!" Daphne cried.

"Girls, he may not be my real grandson," Granny replied, "but I love him like he was my own."

Daphne took her sister's hand and smiled. "I have a feeling we're going to have a lot more to write in those books."

Sabrina scowled.

To be continued . . .

To be continued in

THE SISTERS GRIMM

BOOK TWO

THE UNUSUAL SUSPECTS

ABOUT THE AUTHOR

Michael Buckley is the *New York Times* bestselling author of the *Sisters Grimm* and *NERDS* series. He has also written and developed television shows for many networks. Michael lives in Brooklyn, New York, with his wife, Alison, and his son, Finn.

This book was designed by Jay Colvin and art directed by Chad W. Beckerman. It is set in Adobe Garamond, a typeface based on those created in the sixteenth century by Claude Garamond. Garamond modeled his typefaces on those created by Venetian printers at the end of the fifteenth century. The modern version used in this book was designed by Robert Slimbach, who studied Garamond's historic typefaces at the Plantin-Moretus Museum in Antwerp, Beligium.

The capital letters at the beginning of each chapter are set in Daylilies, designed by Judith Sutcliffe. She created the typeface by decorating Goudy Old Style capitals with lilies.

A GUIDE TO FAIRY TALES
& THE SISTERS GRIMM

Dear Reader,

When I set out to write the adventures of the Sisters Grimm, I wanted to update everyone's favorite fairy-tale characters using adventure, humor, and surprises. I thought it would be easy. After all, I'd heard all the stories and seen all the movies. What else was there to know?

It turns out there was plenty more to know.

When I reread some of the original stories, I found that everything I thought I knew was wrong. Imagine my surprise when I discovered that the Little Mermaid didn't win her handsome prince's heart in the end. Or that Pinocchio wasn't swallowed by a whale but eaten by a shark! Or that Snow White wasn't awakened with a kiss but when a piece of poisoned apple, stuck in her throat, was dislodged. I went back and reread all the classics, by the Brothers Grimm, Hans Christian Andersen, Lewis Carroll, Andrew Lang, Rudyard Kipling, L. Frank Baum, and dozens more. What I found was a wealth of funny, exciting, scary, and adventure-filled stories, and my hope is that the Sisters Grimm series will inspire you to do the same. Your local library should have a wide collection of fairy tales and folklore, filled with as many surprises as there are in Sabrina and Daphne's adventures. I invite you to crack open these classics and find out what you've been missing. Happy reading and beware of the Scarlet Hand!

—Michael Buckley

Fairy Tales

Many people think fairy tales are just stories about princesses and witches that our parents tell us so we won't take candy from strangers or wander off by ourselves. But if fairy tales were only here to teach us lessons, they probably would have disappeared long ago.

Fairy tales tell us big truths about life, not just as it was long ago, but as it is today, and show us how to make our way through it with bravery, cunning, and wisdom. They are such useful guides that they've been followed for centuries, by people in every country on the globe. Two hundred years ago, a young girl fell asleep in her bed listening to the same fairy tale you liked to read when you were little.

So how did fairy tales from so long ago end up here? For a long time, fairy tales were only passed down orally. That means, basically, that they were created from a giant, centuries-long game of telephone. People told stories to children, friends, or strangers they met during their travels. Then those people told the stories to other people, changing little details along the way. The general plots stayed the same, but the stories grew and changed, depending on where and when they were told. Sometimes two different versions of the same story would pop up in two different countries. The names and settings would be different, but the same things would happen. For example, there are versions of the Cinderella story in countries as far apart as Egypt and Iceland!

Following Fairy Tales. The Cinderella story is one of the most famous fairy tales in the world because it's been adapted to so many different cultures and times. The first written version appeared more than a thousand years ago in China, and new versions of the tale pop up all the time—think of all the movies you've seen about a poor, mistreated girl who ends up with the rich, handsome guy. The details change—maybe "Cinderella" works in a car wash or ropes cows—but the plot stays the same.

You can conduct your own experiment to see how fairy tales might grow or change. All you'll need is a piece of paper, a pen, and a few friends.

Have one person start writing two or three sentences on the paper to begin the Cinderella story. Then have that person fold the paper down, so only the last line he or she wrote can be seen.

Pass the paper on to the next person, who will add a few sentences to the story, with only the line before as a guide. Then the second writer should fold the paper again, so that only the last line of his or her writing is visible. Continue to pass the paper, write, and fold until you finish a page, or two if you're feeling ambitious. When you're done, unfold the paper and read the whole story through. See if you can trace how the storyline and characters changed as the story was passed from one person to another.

GRIMMS TO THE RESCUE

For a long time, people told fairy tales by memory, and often stories were changed or even lost as they were passed down. That's when the Brothers Grimm stepped in. Jacob and Wilhelm Grimm grew up in Germany listening to fairy tales, and they worried that the wonderful stories they heard might be changed, lost, or forgotten. The brothers decided to write down their favorite tales so people would remember them forever. Some people think of the Grimm brothers as writers, and they were, but more than writers they were collectors—even hunters—of good stories. They talked to everyone, from their close friends to strangers they met traveling. Once, they met a poor, ragged soldier who asked for their old clothes in exchange for his stories. The Brothers Grimm were more than happy to make the trade—in fact, they probably thought they were getting the better deal!

You may have heard different versions of the same fairy tale, some scarier than others. When the Grimm brothers first wrote their stories down, they were violent tales, packed with villains who died in horrible ways. The Grimms thought that adults, especially professors and historians, would be the ones reading their stories. They were surprised when they realized that it was kids who liked their fairy tales best! So Wilhelm and Jacob rewrote their stories, making them more poetic and a little less violent. But they didn't take everything out, because they knew that being scared was part of the fun of reading fairy tales. They didn't want to cheat their younger readers of a good story.

THE BASIC INGREDIENTS

It seems that an awful lot of fairy tales are full of wicked witches, endangered princesses, and handsome princes who save the day. That's because putting together a fairy tale is kind of like putting together a potion, and different stories use many of the same ingredients. What does a good fairy tale need? Here's a list of some of the most common elements of fairy tales:

> Heroes/good characters
> Villains/very, very bad characters
> Interesting sidekicks
> A journey or quest
> Magic
> A happy ending

Can you think of any other important components of a good fairy tale?

Do you think all of these components are necessary to a good story?

Some fairy tales, like many of the stories written by Hans Christian Andersen, don't end happily. Others, like some more modern renditions of old fairy tales, don't include magic.

As you read *The Sisters Grimm*, look for elements from the list above and see how many you can find. Think of Sabrina, Daphne, and Granny Relda as heroes (or "damsels in distress," sometimes). Who are the villains? Do you ever feel sorry for them? Think about different ways in which *The Sisters Grimm* imitates or challenges the typical fairy-tale formula.

CRIME WATCH

The Grimm sisters are "sleuths of fairy-tale crime." It's a good thing, too, because there seem to be an awful lot of crimes committed in fairy tales. Without the three little (or not so little) pigs out patrolling the streets, crime was rampant throughout many classic fairy tales. Below are some well-known fairy tales and a list of crimes. Can you connect the crime with the story, and bring the perpetrators to justice like the Grimm sisters?

Goldilocks	A	1	Lying
Little Red Riding Hood	B	2	Identity theft
Beauty and the Beast	C	3	Destruction of property
Snow White	D	4	Child labor
Rumplestiltskin	E	5	Hostage-taking
Cinderella	F	6	Attempted murder
The Three Little Pigs	G	7	Breaking and entering

Answers:

A-7 (Goldilocks enters the house of the three bears uninvited)

B-2 (the wolf pretends to be Grandma)

C-5 (the beast makes Beauty stay in his castle and will not let her leave)

D-6 (the evil queen tries to kill Snow White four times)

E-1 (the girl's father lies and tells the king that she can spin gold out of straw)

F-4 (the evil stepmother and her daughters make young Cinderella their slave)

G-3 (the wolf destroys the pigs' houses)

BE THE NEXT GRIMM

Not everybody may get the chance to hang out with Everafters and solve fairy-tale crimes like the Grimm sisters, but anyone can follow in the Grimm brothers' famous storytelling tradition. Because most fairy tales follow a pretty simple formula, it's surprisingly easy to create your own. See if you can use some common building blocks to write your own story. Here are a few questions to get you started thinking:

Who is the hero?

Who is the villain?

Is there a trusty sidekick?

Where does my story take place?

What does my hero want? What is he or she looking for?

What challenges must my hero overcome?

Once you decide what you're writing about, here are some phrases to help you put your ideas all together:

Once upon a time . . .

There once was a boy . . .

Many, many years ago there lived . . .

Now, you shall hear a story that somebody's great-great-grandmother told a little girl many years ago . . .

. . . and _____ was in grave danger . . .

. . . but _____ was too smart to be tricked, and decided to . . .

. . . and they lived happily ever after!

. . . snip, snap, snout. This tale's told out.

Remember, part of the fun of fairy tales is being surprised, so be as creative as you can. Boys don't always have to rescue girls, and villains don't always have to be wicked old women (think about the surprising heroes and villains in the Sisters Grimm books). After you finish your fairy tale, try reading it out loud to see how it sounds. You'll be working in the great, centuries-old tradition of Jacob and Wilhelm Grimm!

TEST YOUR FAIRY-TALE SMARTS

Think you have the smarts to be part of the Grimm family? As Granny Relda teaches, there's lots to learn. See how much you know by taking the following quiz about your favorite tales!

1. The seven dwarfs make an agreement with Snow White allowing her to stay with them if in return she will do what?

a. stand around looking pretty

b. teach them how to wash all the dust off their mining clothes

c. cook, clean, and keep house

d. accompany them to the mines every day and sing while they work.

2. At the very end of Little Red Riding Hood, the wolf's stomach is filled with

    a. Granny's famous chicken wings

    b. Granny

    c. absolutely nothing

    d. stones

3. Before the Queen guesses Rumplestiltskin's real name, she guesses two others, including

    a. Harry

    b. Joshua

    c. Jack

    d. Prince Charming

4. The Evil Sorceress who finds Hansel and Gretel plans to

    a. feed them her leftovers forever

    b. make them clean her house all day long

    c. hold them hostage until their parents pay for them

    d. eat them

5. Rapunzel is raised by an evil enchantress to punish her parents for

    a. exiling the enchantress from their kingdom

    b. stealing some plants from the enchantress's garden

    c. having the fairest daughter in all the land

    d. not taking their daughter to get a haircut when she clearly needs one

Answers: 1-c, 2-d, 3-a, 4-d, 5-b

Original Tales

If you are curious about the original stories collected by the Brothers Grimm and other storytellers from around the world, here's a list of books to start you off, which you should be able to find at your local library:

Andersen's Fairy Tales. Hans Christian Andersen. Wildside Press, 2004.

The Annotated Classic Fairy Tales. Norton, 2002.

The Arabian Nights Entertainments. Andrew Lang. Dover, 1969.

Celtic Folk and Fairy Tales. Joseph Jacobs. Dover, 1968.

Chinese Myths and Fantasies. Cyril Birch. Oxford, 1993.

The Complete Fables. Aesop. Penguin, 1998.

The Complete Fairy Tales of Charles Perrault. Charles Perrault. Clarion, 1993.

The Complete Grimm's Fairy Tales. The Brothers Grimm. Pantheon, 1976.

Demons, Gods, and Holy Men from Indian Myth and Legend. Shahrukh Husain. Schocken, 1987.

English Fairy Tales. Joseph Jacobs. Everyman's Library, 1993.

The Fairy Books. Andrew Lang. Various publishers.

Greek Gods and Heroes. Alice Low. Simon & Schuster, 1985.

Irish Fairy Tales and Legends. Una Leavy. O'Brian Press, 2002.

Italian Folk Tales. Italo Calvino. Harcourt, 1990.

Russian Fairy Tales. Aleksandr A. Afanasiev. Pantheon, 1976.

Spirits, Heroes, and Hunters from North American Indian Mythology. Marion Wood. Knopf, 1982.

Tales of Ancient Egypt. Roger Lancelyn Green. Puffin, 1996.

The Grimm Web

You can find out more about the Brothers Grimm and their stories at these Internet sites:

Brothers Grimm: Fairy Tales, History, Facts, and More
www.nationalgeographic.com/grimm

National Geographic presents twelve tales from the famous brothers in their original form. Open the treasure chest to find a map of the Fairy-Tale Road through Germany, *National Geographic* articles on the Brothers Grimm, links to other Grimm resources, and more.

Grimm Fairy Tales
www.grimmfairytales.com/en/main

Interactive, narrated, animated versions of several fairy tales plus biographical information, games, and other fun stuff from Kids Fun Canada.

The SurLaLune Fairy-Tale Site
www.surlalunefairytales.com

This personal Web site hosted by a librarian serves as a portal to fairy-tale and folklore studies, featuring forty-four annotated fairy tales, with their histories, cross-cultural tales, and illustrations.

Look for
THE COUNCIL OF MIRRORS,
the ninth book in the series!

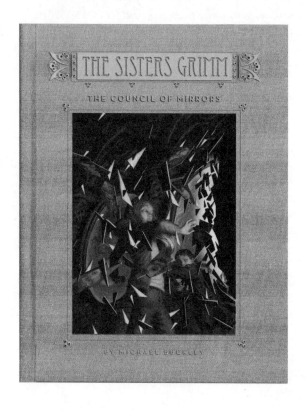

THE SISTERS GRIMM

Catch the magic—

read all the books in Michael Buckley's
New York Times bestselling series!

1 The Fairy-Tale Detectives
978-0-8109-5925-5 hardcover
978-0-8109-9322-8 paperback

5 Magic and Other Misdemeanors
978-0-8109-9358-7 hardcover
978-0-8109-7263-6 paperback

2 The Unusual Suspects
978-0-8109-5926-2 hardcover
978-0-8109-9323-5 paperback

6 Tales from the Hood
978-0-8109-9478-2 hardcover
978-0-8109-8925-2 paperback

3 The Problem Child
978-0-8109-4914-0 hardcover
978-0-8109-9359-4 paperback

7 The Everafter War
978-0-8109-8355-7 hardcover
978-0-8109-8429-5 paperback

4 Once Upon a Crime
978-0-8109-1610-4 hardcover
978-0-8109-9549-9 paperback

8 The Inside Story
978-0-8109-8430-1 hardcover
978-0-8109-9726-4 paperback

Visit www.sistersgrimm.com today!